"Do not be overcome with evil,
but overcome evil with good."
—*Romans* 12:21

This book is dedicated to all the unsung heroes who take a stand against injustice for the sake of others. Many thanks, also, to Joe and Karen for their support and work on my behalf, and to the many faithful readers and friends who keep me in their prayers.

ONE

The keening wails echoing down the usually quiet halls of the Serenity Medical Center made the hair on the back of Samantha Rochard's neck prickle. Every natural instinct told her to flee. Instead, her experience as a registered nurse sent her racing toward the sound of misery.

A doctor, white coat flying behind him, shoved her aside and burst through the curtain into an E.R. exam cubicle. She heard him start to speak. Then, his words were abruptly cut off.

A sixth sense brought Samantha to a skidding halt before the weighted curtain had stopped swinging behind him. Was that scuffling? Fighting? A thud?

She peeked through a slit between the panels. Dr. Weiss, the physician who had elbowed her out of his way, lay on the floor, moaning. A thin, scraggly figure she judged to be male stood with his back to her. The only thing about him that caught her attention and held it was the small, silver-colored revolver he was waving.

Samantha wheeled and flattened herself against a nearby wall. Hands trembling, she pulled out her cell phone, called 911 and cupped her hands around the instrument to muffle her speech.

"We need help at the medical center. Hurry."

"What's the nature of your emergency, ma'am?"

"I don't *know*." Samantha wanted to shout instead of whispering. "I heard a scream and…"

When the dispatcher interrupted to ask, "Is that you again, Ms. Rochard?" she figured her report wasn't going to be taken seriously. So what else was new?

"Look," Samantha said, "we've got a guy in our E.R. with a gun. Isn't that enough?"

"Okay. Stay where you are and let us handle it." There was a rumble of conversation and beeping noises in the background before the dispatcher returned. "We have units on the way. Stay on the line with me."

Samantha was about to reply when someone grabbed a fistful of her shoulder-length, dark hair and jerked her off her feet. The cell phone hit the floor with a splintering crack. She was being dragged backward into the exam area where Dr. Weiss lay!

Her scalp felt as though it was on fire. She couldn't think. Couldn't reason. All she could do was keep screaming "No! No!" and try to regain her balance enough to fight back.

The attacker flung her aside like a sack of dirty laundry. She landed hard. The instant she looked up she knew who had manhandled her. It was one of the teenage Boland boys. *What's his first name? Why can't I remember? Marty, Jimmy, Bobby?* It was Bobby. Bobby Joe. At least that sounded right.

Shying away while her thoughts whirled, Samantha stared at the young man in the tattered jeans and T-shirt. His eyes were wide and darting, their pupils dilated. He was under the influence for sure, which made him even more unpredictable. His demeanor reminded her of an animal caught in the jaws of a steel trap and willing to chew its own leg off to escape.

She licked her lips and found her voice. "Hey, it's me. Samantha Rochard. You're—you're Bobby Joe, right? I used to go to school with your big sisters. Remember?"

His eyes flickered. His body was shaking so uncontrollably his hand kept jerking. The hand with the gun in it. "I—I know," he stammered. "I came to see you 'cause you're a nurse."

"Okay. I'm here," Samantha said with forced

calm. "I'm going to get up now, Bobby. Will you let me do that?"

His nod was quick, twitchy. "Yeah."

Using the edge of the exam table to steady herself she kept her concentration on the teen's face, waiting for him to do something else irrational thanks to his drug-induced paranoia. The biggest plus of the whole situation was the fact that she knew all of the Boland kids had been raised with strong morals and lots of love, even if they hadn't had much else.

Samantha took a deep, settling breath and squared her shoulders. "I'm listening," she told the skinny, long-haired teen. "Why did you want to see me?"

He stepped aside so Samantha could view the occupant of the narrow gurney for the first time. A homemade quilt wrapped a frail, blond child about two years old. The little body lay quiet. Too quiet.

Whipping her stethoscope from around her neck she pushed the teen aside, threw back the edges of the quilt and began to check the child's vital signs. There was a heartbeat! *Thank You, God.*

"What happened?" she demanded.

"I don't know. I was just watchin' him for a friend and…"

"How long? How long has he been like this?"

Instead of answering, the gunman stepped back and began to weep as if his heart was breaking.

Samantha was no longer concerned about anything except the ill child. "Talk to me, Bobby Joe. Tell me everything."

Sobbing was all she heard so she doubled her efforts. "Listen. Time matters. If you think he swallowed something I need to know what and when. Talk to me. Help me save him." She was searching for injuries on the little body as she spoke and finding none.

The young man sank to the floor near Dr. Weiss's feet. Samantha heard him mumble something about a stash and the little boy being too curious. That was enough to get started. She threw aside the curtain surrounding one end of the exam area and found herself staring at a trio of quaking coworkers.

"Narcan," Samantha shouted. "And find me a doctor who's conscious enough to give the order to administer."

"I can do it," Weiss said, rolling onto his hands and knees and pausing before pulling himself erect. He cast a wary glance at the assailant who was still babbling incoherently, then nodded at a middle-aged nurse who stood outside the immediate area. "You. Alice. You heard her. Meds. Stat. And somebody order a chopper. We'll transport to Children's in Little Rock as soon as we stabilize."

"Respirations are slow, pulse rapid and weak," Samantha told him.

"That figures." Weiss blew a sigh. "I'll start an IV while you give him half the dose IM. If the problem isn't opiate-induced, Narcan won't hurt him."

"Right." She administered the injection while other nurses and the doctor worked on the opposite side of the gurney.

The sound of approaching sirens caught her attention. Tensing, she eyed Bobby Joe. He apparently hadn't noticed that the police were almost there.

"Vitals are improving. Somebody take my place for a second," Samantha said before leaving the patient in other capable hands and going to crouch beside the distraught teen.

"We've given the boy an antidote and he's starting to respond. It's going to be okay." Reaching for his weapon and closing her hand around it, she made sure it was pointing in a safe direction, then exerted steady pressure. "You can let go. Give me the gun, Bobby Joe. Everything's under control."

Relieved beyond words when he did as she asked, Samantha stood, holding out the small, silver pistol, butt first and muzzle direction safely diverted, just the way she'd taken it from its owner.

Several police officers were already approaching warily when she turned to face them. Their guns were drawn, their expressions deadly serious so she announced, "You can relax, fellas. Everything's under control. I got his gun away from him for you."

One deputy sidled past her to cuff the addict while another stepped up and took the pistol from her hand.

If Samantha hadn't already been so keyed up that she could barely think straight, she might have shrieked when she saw that cop's face. Her jaw did drop and she was pretty sure her gasp was audible. His light brown hair and eyes and his broad shoulders were all too familiar. It couldn't be him, of course. It simply couldn't be. She hadn't had one of these déjà vu moments for months. Maybe years.

Her pulse leaped as reality replaced imagination. She couldn't catch her breath. This was *not* another bad dream. John Waltham, the man who'd broken her heart so badly she'd wondered if she'd ever recover, was standing right in front of her, big as life.

Before she could decide how to greet him, he set the mood of their reunion. His "What did you think you were *doing?*" was delivered with such force it was practically a growl.

That attitude stiffened her spine and made it easy to answer, "My job."

"You're a nurse, not a cop."

"Oh, so I'm supposed to just stand there while you and your buddies waltz in here and start shooting?"

"If necessary, yes."

"Don't be silly. I knew Bobby Joe wasn't going to hurt me," she insisted, wishing she fully believed her own assertion. When an addict was under the influence there was no way to predict what he or she might do.

Handling the pistol expertly, John unloaded it and passed it to one of his fellow officers to bag as evidence before turning back to Samantha.

She noticed that his expression had softened some but it was too little too late. She was already bristling. "What are you doing back in town?" She eyed him from head to toe. "And why are you dressed like a member of our police force?"

"Because that's what I am. I've come home," he said flatly.

Samantha couldn't believe her ears. After all he'd put her through, all the tears she'd shed after he'd left her high and dry, he had the unmitigated gall to return and go back to work as if nothing had changed. How *dare* he!

Seeing Samantha again had been disquieting to begin with. Seeing her with the perp's loaded gun in her hand had dealt him such a staggering blow he'd almost been rendered speechless.

Although Sam was prettier than ever, she now exhibited an element of authority and expertise that floored him. The last time they'd been together Sam had clung to him, crying and begging him to stay in Serenity. She'd acted as if she couldn't bear to see him go and was positive she couldn't live without him.

Now, however, she was behaving with such self-assurance he was stunned. His high school sweetheart had grown up in his absence. Boy, had she!

Waiting until the addict had been escorted to a patrol car and stuffed into the backseat, John approached her for the second time.

She looked up from her task of packaging the quilt and the child's clothing. She didn't speak, didn't smile.

John cleared his throat. "I think we got off on the wrong foot just now. It's good to see you again, Sam."

All she did was nod.

"Nice job calming the suspect. Just don't try anything like that again."

He'd thought she might reply because her jaw dropped slightly but she snapped it shut and kept mum. "I told you I was sorry a hundred times," he said quietly so others wouldn't overhear. "What happened between us in the past was for the best, Sam. You and I both know that."

With a noisy sigh and shake of her head she regarded him for long seconds before she finally spoke. "I'd adjusted fine to you being a detective in Dallas, John. What the... What are you doing back in Serenity?"

"You don't sound happy to see me."

"Happy? Happy is getting the gun away from Bobby Joe Boland and saving that little boy's life. There was no joy in going through the struggles I faced after you left me. I won't do it again. Not for anything."

Floored, he stuffed his hands into his jacket pockets and tried to look unconcerned. He'd thought he'd made Samantha understand his desire to better himself, to advance his career. Surely she must have had some empathy because she'd insisted she wanted to do the same thing in regard to nursing. They had both succeeded. He'd just had to move away in order to accomplish his goals and she'd been able to do it right there in Serenity.

"I kind of hoped you'd be glad to see me, Sam. It's nice that you're doing so well." He gestured toward the area where the doctor and nurse were smiling at the formerly unconscious boy. "Looks like a good save."

"This time. I wish I could rescue them all."

"Kids, you mean?"

"Yeah." Another sigh. "There are so many like…"

"Like you used to be?" he offered. When her eyes narrowed and she glared at him he was afraid he'd reminded her too much of her own childhood.

"I managed. And I'm still managing," Samantha said, closing and tagging the bag of belongings that would go in the medevac chopper that was going to transport the child to a bigger hospital. "Now, if you'll excuse me, I have work to do."

"Maybe I'll see you in church Sunday?"

You could have knocked him over with a feather when she said, "Not a chance. I don't go to church anymore."

"Why not?" The way John remembered their youth, Sam's faith had seemed stronger than his. What in the world would make her stop attending worship services?

At first he didn't think she was going to answer. When she lifted her chin higher and said, "Because I got tired of everybody asking me about *you,*" he wished she hadn't told him the truth.

The swing shift sped by for Samantha. Weary and eager to get home and relax, she clocked out at midnight, grabbed her purse and headed for her compact, blue sedan.

Overhead lights cast a yellowish glow across the medical-center parking lot. Fall breezes were scattering dry leaves and either piling them against the tires of the few remaining vehicles, or tumbling them down the hill into the farmers' mowed fields beyond.

Samantha turned up the collar of her fleece jacket and clasped her arms across her chest to help ward off the chill. She knew she hadn't been the same since she'd seen John again and she didn't like the feelings of loss—and of buried anger—that kept washing over her.

Logic insisted that it was foolish to relive an unhappy past. The problem was, most of her time with John Waltham had been blissful. Elating. Filled with the promise of a perfect future.

That was the real problem. She was once again coming face-to-face with a shattered dream and seeing how irrational it had been in the first place. Childhood attachments were fine for kids. A person had to grow up eventually. In a way, John had done them both a favor when he'd left town and forced her to stand on her own two feet. Intellectually, she believed that. All she had to do was convince her emotions.

Because of hospital rules, Samantha's car was parked in a distant section of the lot designated for employees. There were some lights back there, too, but the farther she got from the buildings the more forbidding the encroaching darkness seemed.

One hand was inside her shoulder bag, reaching for her keys, when a large, black-clad form stepped out of the shadows. She sensed him before she actually saw him and her fingers began probing the deepest reaches of her purse. Instead of her keys, she gripped a small can of pepper spray.

Shaking on the inside, she continued walking boldly toward her car. When the silent figure blocked her way she simply said, "Excuse me?"

His resulting laugh was far from humorous. Widening his stance he said, "Lady, there is no excuse for the likes of you. Now give it to me."

"I don't know what you're talking about. Move. I need to get to my car." She sidestepped to keep out of reach and raised the spray can, ready to put it to use.

"You think that scares me?" the man said. "I can take that away from you before you know what hit you."

"Why *me?*" she asked, fighting to remain calm enough to defend herself. "I don't know you."

"No, and you won't try to ID me if you know what's good for you. Let's just say we have a mutual friend whose life won't be worth a bucketful of manure if you rat us out." His raspy tone was almost as frightening as the outright threat.

"I don't know what you're talking about. Get out of my way and I'll leave. I won't say a word about this. I promise."

This time his laugh was even more sinister. "You bet you won't. The only way you're getting away from me is if you give me the package."

"*What* package?" She could hear the fear in her voice and rued the lack of self-control.

"The one the Boland kid gave you."

So that was the supposed mutual friend he was threatening to harm. "Bobby didn't give me anything. I hardly *know* him."

"Oh, yeah? Then why did he point to you when they were hauling him off to jail?"

"Me? I didn't even see him leave. He couldn't have pointed to me."

Suddenly, the man lunged.

Samantha directed the pepper spray at his

face and heard him curse as it hit its target but he didn't slow his attack. In the blink of an eye he'd disarmed her and wrenched her purse from her grasp, as well.

Blinding headlights suddenly came out of nowhere and illuminated the darkened corner of the lot. Her head whipped around. A large vehicle, probably a pickup truck, was speeding toward her so fast it looked as though it might actually hit her car or run her over.

Tires screeched on the asphalt. The truck rocked as it slid to a stop. A man in a denim jacket jumped out and raced past Samantha in a blur, hot on the trail of her fleeing attacker.

The whole incident happened so quickly she needed a moment to process the details. What in the world could that guy have meant? Bobby Joe hadn't given her any packages. He hadn't given her anything but a headache. But it was clear the stupid kid was involved with criminals and was in way over his head. Perhaps lethally so.

It quickly dawned on her that the driver of the pickup had looked familiar. Peering after him she saw John Waltham returning with a broad grin and her purse in hand.

Well, now what? she asked herself, trying to still her trembling enough to present a calm facade, even though she'd been scared out of her wits just now. John had saved her from theft and goodness knows what else. She could hardly snub him.

Instead, she merely smiled and said, "Thanks," as she accepted her handbag from him and slung the wide strap over her shoulder.

"You're welcome. Sorry he got away." John eyed the bag. "Aren't you going to check and see if he stole anything?"

"I doubt he had it long enough for that." Samantha nevertheless pawed through the contents. Her wallet and cracked cell phone were still there. To her surprise, so was the pepper spray.

Looking back at her rescuer she raised an eyebrow. "Wait a minute. It's after midnight. What were you doing out here?"

"Waiting for you to get off work so I could try to talk to you again," John said.

"How did you know my hours?"

"I asked at the information desk. That's what they're for. Information, right?"

"They're not supposed to give strangers my personal schedule," Samantha countered.

"Ah, but they could tell I was one of the good guys because I was still in uniform when I asked."

She shivered. "Yeah, well, apparently you weren't the only one waiting for me."

"No kidding. I think I'd better escort you to the station to make a report."

"For a purse snatching? I'd really rather not." *Especially since I don't intend to involve Bobby Joe until I've made sure he won't be hurt worse because of my statement,* she added to herself, considering that decision totally rational under these circumstances.

"Why not?" John was scowling.

"Hey, don't look at me like I'm some kind of criminal. I just don't relish visiting Sheriff Allgood or Chief Kelso, okay? We don't exactly see eye to eye."

John still didn't touch her but he did hover closer, making Samantha feel safer and more secure than she had in a long, long time. "Explain."

She leaned against the side of her car because she was still unsteady on her feet and didn't want him to suspect. "It's not complicated. I see it as my duty to report suspicions of child abuse and the authorities don't often take me seriously. It was bad enough before I became a CASA volunteer but it's even worse now. You know what that is, right?"

"Court Appointed Special Advocates for children? Sure. What's the problem? The people you report are guilty, aren't they?"

"Sometimes. Like Bobby Joe was today."

"And sometimes not?"

"Yeah."

"That's okay, Sam. I understand. You're smart enough to catch clues that others miss."

"Do you really believe that or are you just trying to get back into my good graces?"

"Maybe both. I've been thinking a lot about what you said earlier. It pains me to hear you dropped out of church because of me. Is that actually true?"

"In a manner of speaking. People were so used to seeing us as a couple and expecting us to get…married…that they kept nagging me about it long after you'd left. I finally decided it was easier to stay home than to go through interrogation every Sunday."

"That's a shame."

Samantha knew she'd already revealed too much for her own good so she changed the subject. "If you want me to make a police report I suppose it would be better to get it over with now, while your office is quiet."

She jingled her keys. "I'll take my car. You can follow if you want."

When he smiled tenderly and said, "You couldn't get rid of me tonight if you tried," she was so touched by his evident concern she had to turn away to hide her emotions.

Don't do it, Samantha, she warned herself.

Don't soften. Don't start imagining that you can go back and pick up where you left off. It's far too late for that. The romance is over. Period.

A basic truth struck her as she was climbing into her car. She and John had had more than a romance. They had shared a special friendship for years. And that, more than anything, was what she missed. What she grieved for.

Looking into the side mirror she watched him striding to his truck. There was a time when she'd believed that he was everything she'd ever wanted; that he completed her in a way no one else could.

The lump in her throat and rapid, thrumming pulse told her that she'd never changed her mind. But John had changed his. He had chosen his career over a life with her and the only way she could hope to protect herself from a repeat of the same pain was to guard her heart—no matter what.

TWO

"We could run by Hickory Station for a cup of coffee. They're open all night," John suggested as they left the police station after filing the report.

"It's one o'clock in the morning. I don't need coffee, I need rest." Samantha blew a noisy sigh. "I just want to take my shoes off, put my feet up and veg out."

"Okay. Maybe some other time." His hopes were dashed when he saw the determined expression on her face and the shake of her head.

"I don't think so. Thanks for your help tonight, though."

She offered her hand in parting and he shook it. Her skin was soft as ever although a bit chilly. That wasn't surprising given the outdoor temperature and the incessant autumn wind.

He covered their clasped hands with his free one. "If you ever need anything—anything— just call me. Promise?"

"No. But it's sweet of you to offer." She pulled free, leaving him feeling strangely bereft.

"Do you still live out at the old Prescott place?"

"Yes. I inherited it."

"Good night, then." John raised his arm and waved as she slammed her car door and prepared to drive away. He was going to follow, of course, just to make sure she arrived home safely. Beyond that, there was little he could do other than pray that nothing else happened to endanger her when he didn't happen to be close by.

He wasn't surprised that she'd chosen to stay on at the Prescott farm. The late Elvina Prescott had provided a safe haven and Samantha had loved the elderly lady more than her own kin. When you grew up with a mother who was so emotionally unstable that she abandoned her family, and a father who spent most of his waking hours drunk, it was natural to seek solace elsewhere.

Hanging back, John kept his eyes on the taillights of Samantha's blue compact. As she turned south on Highway 62, he found himself wishing she lived inside the small, close-knit town rather than farther out in the country.

Maybe he could talk her into… *No.* He was the last person Samantha would listen to no matter how much danger she might be in. That was what bothered him the most. Neither of them had recognized her assailant and he'd failed to spot a getaway car, so there was no way to figure out why Sam had been targeted.

John wished he'd thought to ask her if she'd had any other recent run-ins with criminals in the course of her nursing job or as a CASA volunteer. The way she'd described her penchant for reporting possible child abuse she could have made more than one enemy. Matter of fact, she might be the target of multiple irate citizens.

His mind considered various scenarios while he continued to shadow his old friend and marvel at her strong ethics. That was Samantha for you. She had an overblown sense of right and wrong that had gotten her into plenty of trouble as a kid—and apparently she hadn't outgrown it. Like the time she'd stolen a puppy because she'd seen its master beating it.

The memory made him smile. That black-and-brown pup was the ugliest cur he'd ever laid eyes on and maturity hadn't made it any prettier—just a lot bigger. It had scars on its back and a jaw that didn't line up, undoubtedly due to its previous abuse. One eyelid hung perpetually half shut and its odd expression made it look as if it would gladly tear a guy's arm off.

With Samantha, however, the dog had remained as friendly as a puppy and as gentle as a lamb.

Wondering if old Brutus was still alive and kicking, he pictured her playing with the enormous pet while it tried to fit both ends of its gargantuan body onto her lap the way it used to when it was smaller. Sam and the dog had been a perfect match right from the beginning. Both had been unjustly punished and they'd come together to help each other heal.

John pulled to a stop at the end of her long, dirt driveway and watched her car inching up the hill and approaching the farmhouse.

Thankfully, a porch light illuminated most of the front yard. His jaw clenched when he saw her taillights disappear around back. "Come on, Sam. Why didn't you stop in the front where there's more light?"

But she hadn't. And there wasn't a thing he could do about it. He had no business following her in the first place. She'd be within her rights if she reported him for stalking, although he figured he'd be able to talk himself out of trouble due to the recent attack. He could always claim he'd just been passing by and…

John squinted at the house, trying to see more. There was someone moving on the porch! He knew there was. He'd only caught a glimpse of the figure but had no doubts.

Jamming the truck into gear he floored the gas. The rear wheels spun in the dirt and gravel, then caught. He shut off his headlights, willing to take a chance that the driveway to the old farmhouse was as wide and easy to navigate as he remembered from years ago.

Sam was really going to be steamed when he showed up on her doorstep. He just hoped she'd be in good enough shape by the time he reached her to give him a proper dressing-down.

Unwilling to trust the dilapidated old barn to hold up in bad weather, Samantha had paid to have a simple carport built near her back door. It didn't offer the same protection a garage would have, but it was cheap and its metal roof kept hail from denting her car or shattering the windows when bad storms moved through the area.

Weary beyond words she pulled beneath the shelter and parked. By the time she'd opened the car door her canine companion was snuffling at her and wagging his stubby tail.

She scratched behind his ears and patted his broad head. When she asked, "Hi, Brutus. Did you miss me?" she imagined an affirmation in his soft "Wuff."

"Yeah, I love you, too, you old coot," she said, smiling and getting out of the car as best she could while he crowded against her, begging for more attention. "Move it, dog. Mama's tired."

Brutus might as well have been on a short leash because he walked the whole way to the back door with his side rubbing against Samantha's legs, then sat politely at her feet and looked up at her while she unlocked the door.

"Yes, you can come in," she cooed, giving his ears another ruffle. "We'll both have a bedtime snack. How does that sound?"

Still beside her, the dog suddenly turned his head and began to growl. The rumble in his throat was accompanied by a lip-quivering snarl that exposed canine teeth nearly an inch long.

Samantha froze. Listened. Waited for her watchdog to signal what to do next. Her hand lay atop his head and she could feel his whole body trembling.

"What is it, boy? What do you see?"

The dog inched his way around so he was facing the yard and had his broad rump to the door.

As far as Samantha was concerned that made this situation a no-brainer. She quickly stepped into the kitchen and reached for the switch on the wall, then stopped herself. If she flipped those lights on she'd be silhouetted in the open doorway.

"Brutus, come," she ordered. "Come. Now."

Instead of taking his eyes off the yard he literally backed into the house, his nails clicking on the vinyl floor. The minute he was in the clear, she slammed and locked the door.

Although the dog still had his hackles up he seemed to be calming down. Samantha crouched next to him and put one arm around his neck. "I sure wish you could talk. What did you sense, huh? Was it a skunk or an armadillo?"

Rabbits, though plentiful, seldom interested him but he hated skunks and 'dillos. Still, it took quite a bit of incentive to get the old dog going these days. For him to show such concentration and defensiveness meant he was positive something was amiss.

"Okay, Brutus. You win. You can spend the night inside with me," Samantha said with affection. "I don't want to have to wash you in tomato juice because you got skunked. I don't need anything else to make the last twenty-four hours more memorable than they already are."

Suddenly, the dog ducked out of her hold and started to trot toward the front of the house. He barked, but only once. That reaction wouldn't have caused her undue concern if she hadn't just been through the growling spell with him.

He pressed his nose to the crack between the jamb and the heavy, wooden door, snuffling up and down where the door fit the frame the way he did whenever she had a pizza delivered.

Only nobody delivered food at this hour of the morning, not to mention the fact that she hadn't ordered anything.

Grasping Brutus's collar she held tight, leaned close to the door and called, "Who's there?"

When John Waltham answered, "It's me," Samantha didn't know whether to be glad or tell him to scram. Judging by her dog's amiable reaction, at least one of them was happy to encounter him again.

"What are you doing out there? Do you know how much you scared me?"

"If you were scared, it wasn't my fault," John insisted. "Open the door. We need to talk."

Samantha's sense of humor surfaced. *Okay.* If he wanted to come in she'd let him. But she wasn't going to restrain Brutus. If John got knocked down and licked to death, it would serve him right.

She turned on the closest table lamp then reached to unlock the door.

Brutus had reacted with unbridled joy the moment John had spoken and he was still beside himself. He wedged his head into the gap as she started to open the door and shoved with his shoulders, his whole rear half wiggling like his tail.

Anyone other than John might have had trouble getting past a dog so bent on bestowing slobbering affection. Instead of giving ground, however, he simply started forward and Brutus made room.

"I think he remembers me," John said as he shut the door behind him and bent to pet the old dog. "At least somebody is glad to see me."

"He's a dumb dog," Samantha countered, struggling to keep from laughing aloud at the interaction between man and animal. "What does he know?"

"Plenty, if I remember right," John said. "Brutus could always tell the good guys from the bad guys, even when he was a pup." Slipping one hand under the dog's muzzle he lifted his head and smiled affectionately. "He's getting gray. How old is he now?"

"Probably about ten," Samantha said. "I've had him since I was fifteen."

"I remember. I thought you were going to go to jail over that episode, for sure."

The particularly poignant memory sobered her. "I might have if you hadn't arranged to buy him from that awful man who'd been abusing him."

"I didn't get you off the hook all by myself. Mrs. Prescott helped. She convinced the sheriff that you were just doing your civic duty and he had a talk with the guy for us."

"I never knew that."

"There was no need to tell you. Your life was already in an uproar because of your parents and since you were planning to come to live with Mrs. P, she figured it would be good for you to have a pet of your own."

"She was right." Samantha sighed. "So, what was it you just *had* to tell me?"

Straightening, he returned her steady gaze. "I followed you home and…"

"What has gotten into you? I do *not* need a babysitter."

"If you'll stop interrupting, I'll explain."

"Okay, okay."

Reluctant to invite him to make himself comfortable, she nevertheless fell back on her Southern upbringing and gestured toward the tweed-covered sofa. "Have a seat. Can I get you something to drink? Coffee?"

"No, thanks. I'm not staying. I didn't intend to even let you know what I was doing until I thought I saw a shadow moving around on your porch."

"*My* porch?"

"Yeah." Perching on the edge of the couch he continued to pet the dog. "But since Brutus isn't upset, I guess it's nothing."

"But he *was!* Just before he heard you out front he'd been growling at the back door."

John leaped up so fast he nearly knocked the

dog off its feet. "Why didn't you say so in the first place?"

"You didn't ask. Besides, I figured he'd just heard your truck coming up the drive. Relax. That's probably all it was."

"Maybe. Maybe not. Are you sure enough about it to tell me you don't want me to investigate?"

"I didn't say that." Although Samantha was making a silly face at him, there was plenty of fear hiding behind the mock humor. "Go ahead. Knock yourself out."

"Okay. Stay there." Although John was clad in jeans and a denim jacket instead of his uniform, he pulled a small gun from a hidden holster and started toward the kitchen.

Samantha crouched beside her dog and watched her old friend walk away. At least he'd been in the house often enough to know his way around so she didn't need to direct him. The trouble was, she very much wanted to stick closer, and not for *his* sake.

John relied on the living-room lamp for illumination as he edged into the kitchen. His boots clomped hollowly on the floor. He lightened his steps as much as possible but the old house squeaked and groaned like a dilapidated garden gate swinging on rusty hinges.

As his eyes adjusted to the dimness he was able to see well enough to get by. Gun in hand he approached the back door, laid his ear to it and listened. There was nothing to hear. Not even the songs of the usual crickets and night-calling birds. That was a bad sign.

He was about to unlatch the door when he sensed that he was no longer alone. Samantha was creeping up on him quietly enough but Brutus's noisy panting and the click of his nails on the hard floor announced their approach.

"Stay back," John said.

"What did you find? Anything?"

"Not yet. Was this where he was when he growled?"

"Close. We were out on the porch."

"Terrific."

"Hey, don't blame me. I had to get to the house somehow."

"You could have parked in front, under the bright lights."

"That's not where my carport is."

This argumentative exchange was getting them nowhere. It didn't matter what he said, Sam would have a rebuttal ready. She was not making this easier. Then again, she never had been simple to understand, at least not for him. Just when he was certain they saw eye to eye, she'd shock him by proving otherwise or by setting up a no-win situation.

"Look, since you're here, how about unlocking the door and easing it open for me. Just do that and then get out of the way. Can you manage that?"

"Of course."

"Well?" He knew his tone was too harsh but he'd seen her in danger at least twice in the past few hours and that was two times too many to suit him.

He watched her approach in a crouch, hand on the knob, the other on the dog's collar. At least she was thinking clearly enough to keep Brutus out of trouble. Too bad she wasn't that cautious with herself.

"Ready?" Samantha asked, nearly whispering.

John braced himself. "Ready."

She jerked open the door.

Something moved on the other side of the screen.

Startled, John tightened his finger on the trigger for an instant before he realized what he was seeing. A large piece of paper was fluttering against the mesh.

He reached around the screen door frame, grabbed the paper and jerked it loose.

Samantha's voice trembled. "What is it?"

"Looks like a note. Close the door and lock it, then turn on the lights."

His eyes were barely adjusted to the brightness when she rejoined him but he'd already seen plenty. For a brief moment he thought about hiding the details from her, then reconsidered. If Sam was in danger she needed to know everything about the threat.

John holstered his gun, then laid the note on the kitchen counter so they could both study it.

"But out if U know whats good for U" was printed in block letters with broad strokes of a black marking pen.

"Well, they can't spell or punctuate but I get the idea," Samantha said with a short, nervous laugh. "Think I should post the corrected version?"

More than a little worried, John rolled his eyes at her. "No. And we don't want to handle it any more than we have to in case there are fingerprints. What I do think you should do is make a pot of coffee, sit down at the table and tell me who you've made mad lately."

"You act like you think it's a long list."

"Is it?"

"Of course not."

"Okay. I'll go check the rest of the house while you make coffee. Brutus isn't the least bit upset so I assume your prowler is gone but there's no sense taking chances."

He paused at the doorway to the hall and glanced back at her. The dog sat at her feet, leaning his shoulder against her knee, his tongue lolling. "Keep him with you."

Hearing that, Samantha gave a wry chuckle. "Mister, you couldn't separate me from this dog with dynamite."

"No," John said, smiling, "but a slice of baloney might do the trick."

THREE

"I doubt I've had any CASA cases that might still be causing problems," she said, cupping her hands around a steaming mug and watching eddies of cream spread across the surface and lighten the color.

Wishing she'd told John everything her purse snatcher had said, she knew she didn't dare reveal those threats now. Not unless she wanted to listen to another lecture. Besides, there was no reason to assume that the man who had accosted her outside the hospital had left the semiliterate note. It didn't really fit with his verbal warnings.

"Tell me about the cases, anyway. Are any of your CASA assignments recent?" John asked.

"Not really. One was late last year. After that I helped Jill Kirkpatrick—I mean Jill Andrews—and her new husband, Mitch, get set up to adopt the Pearson orphans. I imagine the chief and the sheriff told you all about that murder and kid-napping since it happened so recently."

"Yes. It was my understanding that the guilty parties were incarcerated."

"The instigator has been hospitalized for psychiatric reasons. The others all ended up in jail." She sighed.

"What else? Was that your last case?"

"Nearly. One more concluded several months ago when the court gave the children I was helping to their maternal grandmother."

"Are those parents still around?"

"No. The kids' mother went to jail for unrelated crimes and nobody knows what happened to the father. He split a long time ago."

John nodded. "Okay. So what are you working on right now?"

"Officially, nothing. I have been worried about a seven-year-old boy, Danny Southerland. I'm virtually positive he's being abused. His father works for some kind of investment firm and he's deeply involved in town politics, too. I guess he thinks that makes him above the law."

"Nobody is above the law, Sam. You should know that from personal experience." He reached toward her hand where it rested on the table and tenderly laid his over it.

Samantha's initial urge was to pull away from

him but by the time she had taken a few brief moments in which to relish his warm, gentle touch it was too late. She'd decided to leave her hand right where it was.

"You're just giving back some of the support you got when you needed it," John continued. "All you can do is try your best in any given situation. The results are up to God."

"And to a judge," she added, smiling wistfully. "As far as I know, nobody from CASA is on the Southerland case yet but I understand what you're saying. It's not my job to make things right. I don't have that power."

"Exactly." John leaned back and folded his arms across his chest. "So, tell me more about this Danny. When did you meet him?"

"It all started several months ago." She closed her eyes and pictured the scene in the emergency room. "The last time was the worst. His father brought him to our E.R. because their regular doctor doesn't work on weekends."

"Okay. Go on."

"I asked Mr. Southerland what the problem was and he told me Danny fell. That was his usual explanation."

"What made you suspect abuse? Bruises?"

"Yeah." She took a settling sip from her coffee mug, then continued. "Danny's body language was textbook, too. He was perched on the edge of the exam table with his feet and legs dangling over the side. He wouldn't look up but I could tell he'd been crying. He'd hunched over to cradle his left arm and was holding it tight against his stomach."

"Was it broken?"

"No. I asked him what hurt and he nodded when I touched that arm. One area was showing signs of bruising so I told him the doctor would probably want an X-ray.

"That's when he started to really cry, looked at his father and said, 'It's better. Honest,' as if he was apologizing for getting hurt."

"What did you do then?"

Amazed and filled with relief, Samantha realized that her story was finally being taken seriously. "I said, 'Don't be afraid, Danny. We'll be very careful with your arm.' Then I whispered, 'How did you get hurt?' That's when his father started insisting he fell when he was running in the house. I wasn't too upset until he said it served Danny right to get hurt because he was disobeying."

Nodding, John gave a short chuckle. "I can just picture your reaction to that."

"And you'd be right. If that man had been three times bigger and growling like a grizzly bear I'd still have given him a piece of my mind. I told him that no child deserves to be hurt. Ever."

"What was his response?"

"Nothing. He shut up the minute Dr. Weiss came into the cubicle."

"Did he ever threaten you?"

"No. When I got the doctor alone later, and suggested we report possible abuse, he laughed at me. It seems Weiss and Ben Southerland go to the same church. Not only that, the man is about to be appointed to the medical-center board. The doctor swears there's no way an upstanding citizen like that would abuse his son."

"What about his wife? Would she…?"

"I don't know. I was told flat out that it was an accident and ordered to forget it."

John's brow furrowed. "Wait a second. If nobody reported him, why should the guy be mad at you?"

Knowing her cheeks were betraying embarrassment, Samantha forged ahead. "Because I went against the doctor's orders and called in a report. I had to, you know, even if my bosses fired me over it."

"Good for you."

She huffed. "That's not how the police responded. They acted like they thought I was crazy. Maybe I have been wrong a few times in the past, but not this time. I know an abused kid when I see one, even if I can't prove it."

"Did you ask that your identity be kept secret when you made your report?"

"Are you joking? In Serenity? Around here, the only difference between normal conversation and deep, dark secrets is how long it takes the news to travel. Besides, considering my reputation and the fact that I was working E.R. that day, there wouldn't be much doubt where the complaint originated."

"I suppose you're right." John got to his feet, carried his mug to the sink and rinsed it out. "I'd better hit the road. Are you going to be okay if I go?"

"Sure. All I have to do is figure out who wanted me to butt out of their business. Piece of cake."

He turned and leaned against the edge of the counter, crossing his arms over his chest. "I just had a thought."

"If it means I'll have to quit defending kids and keep my mouth shut when I see a problem, forget it."

"Nothing of the kind. I was just thinking about maybe keeping an eye on Danny and his family—in a casual way, of course."

"How do you propose to do that? You don't even know what they look like."

"No, but you do. What church does Dr. Weiss go to these days? Seems to me I used to see him at Serenity Chapel when I still lived around here."

It was Samantha's turn to scowl. "Oh, no, you don't. You're not going to coerce me into going to church again. I told you I gave that up."

"You won't reconsider? Not even for Danny's sake?"

"That's cheating, Waltham. You know I'd do just about anything to protect kids."

"Sure do. So, is it a date or do you have to work this coming weekend?"

Disgusted at the way she'd walked right into his verbal trap, Samantha made a face. "No date. But I will consider going since I'm not on duty. For Danny's sake."

"Of course."

Judging by the way John was beaming he was more than satisfied. Well, let him gloat. Even if she did give in and attend a Sunday service or two, that wouldn't change anything between them.

It wouldn't change anything between her and God, either, Samantha told herself. She had prayed and prayed for the Lord to intervene and keep John from abandoning her and what had happened? Nothing. Absolutely nothing. John had packed up and headed for Texas as if her feelings, her tears, hadn't mattered to him one little bit.

Was she giving the obstinate man too much of a place in her current affairs? She did need an ally. And he was the only person who seemed to believe her. Therefore, she could not, in good conscience, dismiss his offer of assistance. What she could do, would do, was keep her emotional distance from him. Beginning now.

"If I do decide to go back to church—and I'm not saying I will—it'll be by myself. The last thing I want is for people to think of us as a couple again. It's taken me years to get them to stop asking how you are. As if I knew."

"I did email and send you updates after I left," he countered.

"For a few months."

"You never answered me. Not once. What did you expect me to do?"

She wasn't about to tell him that every time she'd gotten a message from him, it had sent her formerly upbeat mood sinking into a bottomless pit of despair and self-pity. In a way, it had been a relief when he'd stopped trying to communicate.

"I didn't expect anything," Samantha said. "You made yourself perfectly clear when you decided to leave." Although she knew her words had an argumentative edge she didn't seem to be able to control herself. It was as if John brought out both the best and the worst in her.

It was a definite relief when he smiled again instead of joining the quarrel and said, "Speaking of leaving..."

Samantha was instantly contrite. "Thank you for looking out for me tonight. I guess I didn't sound grateful just now but I am. Really."

"I know." He paused and bent to pet Brutus who promptly plopped down and rolled over to beg for a tummy rub.

"Apparently, so is my dog," she quipped. "I'm surprised he remembered you after such a long time."

"Hey, we were good buddies," John said, straightening and pulling his jacket on before reaching into his pocket and handing her a generic police department card. "My private cell number is on the back. If you have any more problems, call me."

"I keep telling you I can take care of myself. I've been doing it for a long time."

"Yes, but you didn't have a prowler leaving threatening notes on your door or a purse snatcher grabbing you." His eyes narrowed. "You don't see any connection, do you, Sam?"

"Of course not." Loath to admit she might actually need help someday, she nevertheless accepted the card.

"Do you have a cell phone?" he asked.

"I did, until this afternoon when Bobby Joe made me drop it. I'll get another one ASAP."

"When you do, I want that number."

Facing him, hands on her hips, she shook her head slowly. "You're really getting bossy. You of all people ought to know that approach doesn't work with me."

"I'd apologize if I thought I was in the wrong," he countered, still grinning and giving the dog's head a parting pat as he headed for the front door. "Since we both know I'm not, I'll just leave before you can think of some other reason to throw me out."

"Good plan." A smile twitched at the corners of her mouth until she gave in and released it. "Good night, Officer Waltham."

He tipped an imaginary cap and bowed. "Good night, Ms. Rochard. Lock this door after me."

"Bossy."

"But *right*," he countered, sobering. "And you know it." The door slammed, punctuating his parting comment.

As Samantha turned first the lock, then the dead bolt, she realized there had been another possible meaning to his words. Had the strange look on his face at the instant he'd shut the door meant he'd realized it, too, or had he simply been needling her the way he always used to?

Years ago, when her life had seemed perfect and complete, John had often insisted how *right* they were for each other. That memory was so crisp, so poignant, it brought a catch to her breath and tied her stomach in a knot until she managed to calm herself with common sense.

Of course he hadn't meant anything personal. Why would he? Their romance was ancient history. If he thought she'd waited five whole years pining away for him, he had another think coming. She was over her crush on that disgusting man.

Period. End of story.

Samantha had spent Friday and Saturday nights jumping at every creak of the old house and obsessing over whether or not to attend church. When she'd finally grown weary enough to quit imagining some crazed criminal bursting into the bedroom and attacking her, she'd dozed fitfully, trusting her dog to keep watch.

By Sunday morning, she was ready to accept John's challenge. For Danny's sake, of course.

She chose a slim, black skirt and a silky blouse with warm fall colors that she'd bought after John had left town. The last thing she wanted to do was dredge up old memories by wearing something he had once admired.

Brutus had begged to be let out the front door first thing that morning and had returned promptly to resume his usual napping, so she decided to leave him dozing peacefully next to her favorite chair, knowing she wouldn't be gone for very long.

Unduly nervous and not sure why, Samantha finally quit fidgeting, grabbed her Bible and her purse and headed for her car.

Securing the kitchen door behind her, she fisted her key ring and turned around. That's when she saw it.

"My car!"

Her jaw dropped. Her heart began to race. All four doors gaped open. Stuffing and small pieces of fabric lay scattered in the dirt. She didn't have to look closely at the opposite side to figure it was the same. Someone had ripped the seats to shreds!

Suddenly aware that she was standing there totally exposed and unprotected, she laid her Bible on the porch railing and instinctively reached for her cell phone. The smashed one. The useless piece of plastic that she had failed to replace in a timely manner.

Hopeful, she flipped it open just the same. It was dead. Worthless. "*Now* what?"

Thinking of how vehemently she'd insisted that she didn't need watching, she wished she'd been a little less self-assured. It was one thing to tell John that she could take care of herself when she had transportation and communication. It was quite another to be standing there staring at her gutted blue compact and belatedly remembering that her phone didn't work, either.

The most natural thing to do was return to the house and lock herself in but that would mean giving up. Letting the bad guys win. Plus, she'd be a virtual prisoner.

Knees weak, body trembling, Samantha scanned the yard and tried to assure herself she'd be okay. Nothing was moving. There were no hulking figures dressed in black and no monsters peeking from behind the old barn doors.

Brutus hadn't made a sound when she'd let him out that morning, either. Therefore, whoever had ravaged her car must be long gone. She hoped.

Did somebody think something was hidden in the car, like maybe the mysterious package her assailant had insisted she'd had?

"That doesn't make any sense," she muttered, slowly descending the stairs and creeping closer to the car, purse slung over her shoulder, Bible in the crook of her arm, pepper spray at the ready in her other hand.

Up close the upholstery was a worse mess than she'd thought, except for the driver's seat. There were several slashes in it as well, but all the stuffing hadn't been pulled out.

That was good enough for Samantha. The house was secure and her watchdog was on duty. The smartest thing for her to do was get into the car and leave, as planned, so she could report the vandalism from a working phone.

"I'll be fine," she insisted, trying to convince herself she meant it.

The rear doors of the car and the trunk lid stood open, as did the front passenger door. Samantha would have shut them all before leaving, but something told her it was smarter to try to start the engine first. If it, too, had been tampered with she wanted to stay as close to the house as possible.

Brushing aside bits of stuffing and tossing her purse, Bible and the pepper spray in ahead of her, she slid behind the wheel. Fit the key into the ignition. Turned it.

The motor had always started easily. Not this time. It coughed as if it were choking.

Samantha's heart lodged in her throat. Had they disabled her car so she couldn't flee? Was she their real target? Were they out there, hiding, waiting for her to show herself before they pounced?

Something near the barn caught her attention out of the corner of her eye but when she swiveled to look, there was nothing unusual to see. Had there been? Or was she imagining threats simply because she was already so frightened she could barely think, barely breathe?

One more try. She'd give the car one more chance to start, then bolt for the house and try to get the door open before anyone had time to catch her.

She turned the key and pumped the accelerator. The car coughed. It started!

There was the shadow again. Only this time it was passing her rearview mirror! She shifted into gear. Saw an arm reaching for the open door. Floored the gas and hoped it would be enough.

The engine sputtered again before starting to race.

"Come on, come on," Samantha shouted, as if the car could hear and obey.

Wonder of wonders, it began to pull away.

She heard a guttural shout behind her that morphed into a chain of curses.

This was no time to stop and close the car doors or the trunk. Not if she intended to make good her escape.

Hands fisted on the wheel, car careening down the dirt road with the trunk lid flapping and the unlatched doors opening and closing erratically, Samantha could hardly believe that she'd gotten away.

Or had she? A dark-colored pickup truck was stopped by the bank of rural mailboxes that served her immediate area.

As she drew nearer, it pulled out. One threat lay behind her and another now completely blocked the narrow road ahead.

She was trapped!

FOUR

John saw Samantha's car approaching. He wouldn't have thought much about her excessive speed if he hadn't seen the condition of the vehicle she was driving. Its doors were flapping like the wings of a wounded duck and every time Samantha hit a bump, the trunk lid bounced erratically.

There was no way he was going to let her pass and continue to town when her car was obviously unsafe. He eased forward into the roadway and blocked her exit.

For a few moments it seemed as if she was going to ram his truck. Her tires threw up clouds of dust and gravel as she finally applied the brakes and started to skid.

John braced himself, ready for impact. It didn't come. Instead, Samantha bailed out of her car and started to sprint away.

He stepped down from the cab of the pickup and hollered, "Hey, Sam! Hold on. It's just me."

In the seconds it took for her to come to her senses he saw no change in her actions. Then, as if in slow motion, she wheeled and came straight at him. Instead of slowing her pace, however, she barreled into his chest so forcefully it staggered him.

He grasped her upper arms and held her away so he could look her in the eyes when he asked, "What's going on?"

"My—my car. Somebody ransacked it."

"Why are the doors open?"

She was gulping air, fighting to catch her breath. "Be-because…"

"Okay. Calm down. I've got you," John said, wrapping her in a tight embrace and steadying them both against the side of his truck. "Take your time."

While both her arms encircled his waist and her cheek lay against his chest, she continued to try to explain.

"At the house. A man. Coming at me. I didn't have time to…"

"Just now? You saw a prowler just now?"

Samantha nodded, lifting her head. "Uh-huh."

"What did he look like?"

"It was a big shadow. I know somebody was after me."

"Maybe you imagined it."

As she eased away from him and looked up into his eyes, she was shaking her head. "No way. I may have a good imagination but I've never heard one of my daydreams curse before."

That was enough for John. He ushered her into his truck and closed the door before using his cell to call the station with a report.

In case there was anyone leaving Sam's he wanted to be in place to at least get an ID. If nobody came by, that would be okay, too, because it would mean that whoever had trashed her car was still up there.

Only one dirt drive led in and out. Anyone who had been present when she'd left the house had a choice of trying to flee past him or being discovered by the officers he'd summoned.

Either way, he won. And so did Sam.

Sirens broke the peaceful, Sunday morning silence. Samantha shivered, glad when John slipped his arm around her shoulders.

"Take it easy. It's almost over."

"Oh, yeah? Says who?"

He gave her a quick squeeze. "Says me. I'm always right, remember?"

"I remember that you *thought* you were," she countered. "I'll reserve judgment."

"Some things never change, do they, Sam?" He chuckled. "Think about this situation. You said you saw someone up at your house. There's only one way in and out and we're parked in the road. Therefore, whoever was up there before is still there, the cops will catch him and your troubles will be over. Simple."

"I hope you're right, but…"

"But you can't believe I can be? That's hardly a surprise," he said flatly as he removed his arm from her shoulders and prepared to get out of the truck to meet his fellow officers.

He hesitated only long enough to gesture in a blocking motion. "You stay put. I'll be back as soon as I've briefed Glenn and Walter."

If Samantha hadn't been so shaky she might have argued or at least tried to follow. Unfortunately, her knocking knees didn't feel ready to support her, let alone help her pretend she hadn't been terrified.

This is ridiculous, she reasoned, angry with herself. Here she was, an independent, capable career woman who had handled her private life just fine until John Waltham had returned to Serenity.

Was he the *real* problem? She couldn't accept that theory without reservations. Not when so many outside influences seemed to be in play. Even without John she would have been accosted in the hospital parking lot and her car would have been vandalized. Perhaps it was time she confessed everything the purse snatcher had said.

That conclusion brought a deep sigh. Yes. It was not only time, it was long past the time when she should have told the authorities the whole story. There was only so much she could do to protect the Boland boy, and she certainly didn't want to become his enabler by letting him get away with criminal activities.

Fully decided, Samantha scooted across the seat, opened the passenger door and slid out. She paused to make sure her legs would support her well enough before trying to follow John.

The older, taller, gray-haired member of the team he'd been speaking with pointed in her direction as she approached. Since she knew both men she greeted them with a smile. "Morning, Walter. Good to see you."

The cop who was closer to her age removed his hat, ran his palm over his blond crew cut and blushed slightly when she added, "Hi, Glenn."

John whirled to face her, his brow furrowed and his jaw set firmly. "I thought I told you…"

"I know, I know. But there's one more thing you should all know before you go looking for the vandal who trashed my car."

Now that she had everyone's undivided attention she found her mouth excessively dry and her words hard to form. "Um, it's like this," she began, staying focused mostly on Walter because she saw him as the least likely to chastise her. "I may know what the guy who tore up my car was after."

John stared through narrowed eyes. "Go on."

"That night, when that man snatched my purse, he mentioned something about a package Bobby Joe Boland was supposed to have given me. I don't have it, of course, but apparently somebody thinks I do."

The look on John's face was far darker than that of his companions. While the other two officers merely nodded and Glenn made notes, John was clearly fighting to control his rising temper.

"You didn't say a thing about this that night."

"I—I guess I forgot."

"You always were a lousy liar," he countered before turning to the others. "Okay. Now this whole thing is starting to make sense. I can stay here and continue to block the road if you want. Just be careful. Boland was into drugs so this prowler is probably frantic to get his hands on whatever stash the kid was carrying before he was arrested at the hospital."

Samantha was sorry to see the others nod, get back into their patrol unit and start for her house. That meant she was alone with John. And with his temper.

When he turned back to face her, he looked more irate than she had ever seen him. That impression was so strong it caused her to cringe when he reached toward her.

"I'm not going to hurt you, Sam," he said, dropping his hand to his side and shaking his head soberly. "I'm not like your father, okay?"

"I know."

"Then stop looking at me as if you expect me to start yelling and swinging."

"Sorry. Old habits die hard."

"That, they do." A smile lifted the corners of his mouth but the emotion didn't quite reach his eyes.

He offered his hand to her, waited a few heartbeats then started to pull back.

Samantha moved quickly to grasp it before he could change his mind. The feeling of safety and concern in John's tender touch was all-encompassing and so comforting it nearly brought tears to her eyes.

Holding his hand like this was dumb. Foolish. Ridiculous, given their stormy history. It was also something she was not ready to relinquish. Not yet. Not when the police were still at her house searching for her erstwhile attacker.

The phone in John's pocket jingled and he flipped it open to answer. "Waltham."

Samantha's pulse was hammering in her ears

so loudly she could hardly hear anything else. The expression on her companion's face was enough to tell her the officers had not found a prowler.

"Okay," John said into the phone. "We'll be right up. Don't go into the house until we get there. She's got a watchdog the size of a pony inside."

He ended the call and started toward his truck, still holding her hand and dragging her along so fast she had to practically jog to keep pace.

"What is it? What did they see? There has to be someone up there. I know there does."

"Not now," John said, sounding cynical. "They spotted tracks from an all-terrain vehicle. Looks like your prowler made his getaway on an ATV."

"I didn't hear anything like that, did you?"

"We probably wouldn't have when we were both concentrating on your wild driving. Apparently, while you were going one way, your druggie friend was headed in the opposite direction. He could be miles away by now."

"I certainly hope so," Samantha said. She scooted into the truck on the driver's side, then slid over to make room for John.

The grim look he shot in her direction was unsettling. Nervousness kept her talking. "What?

You don't want him to go away because you want to capture him? I get it, believe me. What I meant was I hope I never see him or his cronics again."

"That's not likely," John warned. "As long as they think you took some kind of package from the Boland kid they'll keep coming after it. And you."

"What can I do? I told you, Bobby Joe didn't give me a thing."

"Is that the truth?"

She bristled. "Of course it is."

John's smile grew sardonic, as if he wanted to believe her but couldn't quite manage it in spite of his earlier claim that she was a poor liar. She could sort of understand that point of view. Perhaps it was time for a more detailed explanation of her motives.

"I would have gotten around to telling you about what the purse snatcher said," Samantha insisted. "Honest I would. I was just worried about Bobby getting in more trouble because of me. I know his whole family. He's not a bad kid at heart."

"He's an addict who probably sells the stuff to innocent little kids to support his habit. Is that the way you want to take care of the children in Serenity?"

"Of course not. I was planning to talk to

Bobby's folks but I wanted to wait and see what the actual charges were before I said anything, that's all. This whole drug-conspiracy idea might be nothing more than a big misunderstanding."

"Even if it is, there's still somebody out to get you, Sam. All the good intentions in the world won't protect you from evil if you don't use your head."

"Humph. I thought you believed in God taking care of His own."

"I do. But I also know He gave us brains and expects us to think with them. I may be a Christian but I still put bullets in my gun. It would be idiotic not to."

"Okay, you've made your point."

She settled back against the seat as John started the truck and headed up the hill toward the old farmhouse. He was right, of course. It made perfect sense to use the capabilities each of them had been given. That was what she was doing when she volunteered through CASA. And that was the same thing John had been doing when he'd put himself in place to protect her.

That action wasn't out of the ordinary. It was merely what he did. Who he was at heart. He would have done the exact same thing for anyone he felt was in danger.

Her conclusion about not being special to him was so obviously correct, it hurt.

First out of the truck, John trusted the other officers to have done their jobs so he didn't order Sam to stay put. His opinion seemed to have little effect on her and the way he saw it, the less he tried to control her unnecessarily, the less they'd butt heads.

It didn't surprise him that she was at his elbow when Walter showed him the tire tracks. John crouched. "They're from an ATV, all right. There are probably hundreds just like this in Fulton County. You got pictures?"

"Yep. Measurements, too." The grizzled, older man's attitude clearly showed a chip on his shoulder. John understood. He'd returned to his former hometown with a degree in law enforcement and big-city experience that Chief Kelso had bragged of as an asset when he'd reintroduced him to the men he'd be working with. Given the fact that they had remained local and he was now viewed as an outsider, it was normal for them to feel a little put out.

"I'm sure you did everything by the book," John assured him. "How about footprints?"

"It's pretty dry and dusty. Not much to see."

"Okay. We'll put the dog out and let you in."

"House is locked. I already tried the door."

"Right." He looked to Samantha. "You'll need to open the door for us."

Eyes widening, she stared at the porch. "Oh, no. My keys are still in the car. So is my purse."

"Okay." John rolled his eyes and sighed noisily. "Wait here with Glenn and Walter. I'll be right back with your stuff."

There was no way he would have considered leaving her at the farmhouse if she hadn't had the companionship of veteran officers. They might look and act like good old boys most of the time but they were both plenty sharp. Sam would be safe with them, at least for the few minutes it would take him to retrieve her keys.

John made the trip down the hill quickly and easily. Stopping next to Samantha's car he left his truck idling and stepped out. Everything looked the same as it had earlier.

He leaned in and reached around the car's steering column, expecting to find the keys dangling from the ignition. That slot was empty. So where were her keys? Had Sam dropped them when she'd bolted?

Scowling, he squinted at the floor mats, then probed the slashes in the messy seat, finally scanning the bare ground outside the car. No keys. No purse, either. There was nothing left in Sam's car but a worn, leather-covered Bible.

John straightened and carefully studied his surroundings. Had there been time for whoever had left the house on the ATV to have circled around and cleaned out the car? Maybe. Maybe not. It hardly mattered how many thieves were involved at this point. Someone had stolen everything except Sam's Bible, including the keys to her house.

If the criminals came back, and John was positive they would, they could simply unlock her doors and walk in. Not only was Samantha in worse danger than before, it was at least partially his fault.

Samantha could tell from John's closed expression and stiff body language upon his return that all was not well. The moment she saw him climb out of his truck and start toward her carrying her Bible, she assumed that that was the only thing he'd managed to retrieve.

"My purse?" she asked, trying not to sound as if she were making any kind of accusation.

"No sign of it. This was all there was left in the car," he said, handing her the Bible. "I'm sorry. I should have made sure you had all your things with you before we came up here. I wasn't thinking clearly."

"I wasn't, either." The unshed tears that misted

her vision were unacceptable. She blinked them away. "I'm sorry to cause all these problems."

"It's not like you went looking for trouble. At least not this time."

Samantha was relieved to see a smile start to tease one side of his mouth when she said, "Thanks, I think."

The more John's expression softened, the easier it was for her to begin to smile at him—and at the other officers. "So, gentlemen, what do I do next?" She checked her watch. "I see we're already too late for church."

"Maybe we'll take in the evening service," John said. "Do you still hide a spare house key in the old barn?"

"Yes! I'd forgotten all about that. I'll go get it."

"No. I'll go. You stay out here with Walt."

"It's on a nail, just inside the door to the left." Samantha wasn't about to argue with John this time. The notion of having her private space invaded so easily gave her the creeps. In mild weather she liked to throw open all the windows to let in fresh air. That practice was probably going to have to stop, at least temporarily. Moreover, she'd need new locks on her doors, not to mention doing something about changing the ignition, door and trunk locks in her car. This was getting complicated. And worse by the minute.

Returning with the single key, John unlocked the door and controlled Brutus's exit so the other officers could enter the kitchen.

The mostly black dog bounded off the back porch and gamboled up to greet her. Just as delighted to see him, she bent to stroke his broad head and rusty-colored eyebrows, then ruffled his darker ears, speaking soft encouragements and enjoying the uncomplicated companionship while she bided her time.

"I am glad about one thing," Samantha told John when he finally rejoined her. "They didn't hurt Brutus. They could have. I let him out the front door this morning and if he'd realized someone strange was in the backyard he might have gone after them. No telling what they'd have done to him then."

"Really? He was outside earlier?"

"Of course. No way was I going to leave for the morning without giving him a chance to go out first."

"Just making sure."

Judging by the way her old friend was scowling at her he had come to some conclusion. Since he didn't seem inclined to share his thoughts she decided to probe for answers.

"Okay. I can see the wheels turning in your brain, Waltham. So, give. What are you thinking?"

"A couple of things. First, if Brutus was outside and the perp was still hanging around, why didn't the dog alert?"

"Good question. Are you saying you think he recognized somebody?"

"It's certainly possible. Have you had any work done around this place recently? For instance, did you hire any handymen, any strangers?"

"No. None." She sighed thoughtfully. "Brutus may be an old dog but you saw how well he remembered you. If he did notice someone messing with my car it didn't have to be anybody he'd recently met. He's with me whenever I run errands and he always attracts plenty of attention. He probably knows at least half the people in town."

"True."

"You said you'd thought of a couple of things. What else?" When John stepped closer and leaned in to speak more quietly she immediately sensed the gravity of what he was about to say.

"Okay. Since your car had already been thoroughly ransacked, why did the man or men stick around? Why didn't they make their getaway long before you came out of the house?"

"How should *I* know?"

"Think carefully, Sam. Whoever vandalized your car was waiting."

He paused and lightly touched her shoulder before he added, "Waiting for you."

FIVE

He'd hated to be so blunt, to purposely frighten her, but as John saw it, there was no other way to make Samantha take his warnings seriously enough. She'd lived her whole life in this same small town. That made her both naive and overly complacent. He was neither.

Noting her lingering expression of astonishment he slipped an arm lightly around her shoulders and gave her a friendly squeeze. "Don't worry, Sam. I'll stick around until things settle down for you."

When she replied, "That's what I'm afraid of," he had to grin.

"I see you haven't lost your sense of humor."

"More like my sense of irony," Samantha quipped back. "Has it occurred to you that everything that's been happening has been contrary to what I told you when you first showed up?"

"You mean the part about not wanting me

around? Yeah, I did think of that." It was a struggle for him to keep smiling when what he wanted to do was pull her closer and promise to keep her safely by his side indefinitely. "Don't worry. I know you're only tolerating me because you need protection."

She made a silly face and arched her brows. "I wouldn't put it that bluntly. I'm not trying to be cruel."

"I know you're not." John's smile returned in full and he could feel his pulse starting to speed, meaning it was high time he released her and stepped away.

"Okay. What do we do now?"

"As soon as Walt and his partner finish searching your house you need to get in touch with your credit-card companies and cancel all the cards that were stolen."

"Um, okay. Any chance I can borrow your cell phone? Mine bit the dust, remember?"

"Right. I'll drive you over to Ash Flat later and you can pick up another phone. We'll need new lock sets for your front and back doors, too. The car will need to be towed in and checked for prints before we do anything else with it."

"We?"

"Yes, we. Get used to it, Sam. After I advise Chief Kelso of your problems I imagine he'll let me hang around. At least I hope so."

"What about asking Adelaide Crowe to keep me company? You remember her, don't you? She's a sheriff's deputy now. I worked with her on one of the CASA cases I told you about."

That suggestion, sensible though it was, hit John like a punch in the stomach. "You really do want to get rid of me, don't you?"

"I didn't say that. I was just thinking it would be easier on both of us if we weren't forced to spend so much time together."

Forced? Shrugging, he had to accept her logic. "All right. I'll look into it Monday morning and see if your house is within her jurisdiction. In the meantime, do you think you can grit your teeth and put up with me a little while longer?"

Samantha's widening smile and the twinkle in her dark eyes lifted his spirits even before she said, "I guess I can manage. And in case I didn't mention it earlier, thanks again for rescuing me, Officer Waltham."

He smiled back at her. "Actually, it's *Detective,* although I don't plan to ask anyone to use my rank, at least not until I've been here long enough to feel accepted."

"You don't think you are?"

"No. I was gone too long. Too much has changed. I can't say I blame the men who stayed behind for being a little jealous."

Samantha's smile began to wane and she glanced toward her back door, obviously deep in thought. When she arched a brow, cocked her head and asked, "Is there any chance one of the guys you work with might be stirring up trouble to try to discredit you?" he was floored.

Being a veteran of undercover work, he was able to mask his surprise. At least he hoped he was. "No way. I've known all those men since before I went away. I do wish the chief hadn't insisted on reciting my credentials and experience in front of everyone after he hired me, but that's no reason for longtime police officers to start pulling pranks."

"Pranks?" Samantha faced him, hands fisted on her hips. "Are you saying what happened to my poor car was some kind of stupid *joke?*"

"Not at all. We're talking about two totally different things here."

"I disagree. Whatever began with Bobby Joe is still going on. Whether or not some of your fellow officers may be throwing in false clues to drive you crazy is a fair question. I doubt old Walter would give you grief but I can't believe all cops are as upstanding as you are."

The sound of the back door screen slamming kept John from the rebuttal he'd intended to give. There was no way any of the men he worked with would be mixed up in actual crime, although he wouldn't put it past them to conduct a little harmless hazing. Samantha was right about that. He just didn't intend to let her influence him against men he had to rely upon day after day.

He left her and approached the others. "Find anything?"

They both shook their heads.

"Okay. Make arrangements with whoever you usually use to have Samantha's car towed and impounded. We'll finish up here and then I'll bring her to the station."

Glenn winked at him before glancing past to focus on Sam. "Sure you don't need a little help here, Detective? I'm happily single again. I'd be glad to pitch in and give you a hand."

Although John felt an instant surge of animosity he hid his ire behind a casual smile. "Thanks for the offer, buddy. I'll keep it in mind in case this victim starts to give me too much grief."

"You do that." Glenn touched the brim of his cap as he sauntered past Samantha and bid her goodbye with a simple nod and a pleasant, "Ma'am."

John shook hands with Walter. "Thanks for your help."

"Just doin' my job." The older man eyed his partner. "Don't mind him. He's been like that ever since his wife left him. A real pain in the…"

"No problem," John said flatly, "as long as he keeps his mind on his work."

Walter hooted as if he'd just heard the punch line to a great joke. "Yeah, well, see that you do the same. You may have a fancy diploma that says you're the smartest detective since Sherlock Holmes but around here you're just one of the boys."

"I know that. It's what I wanted when I came back to Serenity. I'd have hired on with the Sheriff's Department again if Harlan had had an opening."

Obviously highly amused, Walt chuckled. "Okay, suppose I buy that, and I'm not sayin' I do, how come you're always first on scene when something bad happens to Ms. Rochard? You tryin' to tell me that's pure coincidence?"

"No." John spoke aside. "I stumbled into this mess when I responded to the hostage crisis at the hospital. Ever since then I've been keeping an eye on her on my own time."

"You wouldn't be tryin' to get back into her good graces by settin' her up so you can pretend to rescue her, would you? 'Cause if I found out you were, I'd have to report you."

Sobering and shaking his head John assured the veteran cop that his intentions and actions were honorable. "All I'm trying to do is prevent another crime." He raised his right hand. "I swear it."

"Okay. But just you remember that Samantha is one of ours. Always was, always will be. If someone was to try to hurt her I'd be the first one in line to even the score."

"Right after me," John vowed. "Thanks for your concern. I feel better knowing you and I are on the same page."

Watching the others drive away, John returned to Samantha.

She arched a brow. "What was all that about?"

"Man talk."

"Oh? Then why did Glenn leer at me and why did Walt look as if he was thinking about punching you in the nose?"

"Let's just say that I no longer worry about either of them causing your problems. Glenn wants a date and Walt warned me that I'd better not do anything to hurt you."

Although Sam was still smiling when she said, "Where was he five years ago?" John could tell there was far too much truth behind her candid comment.

The trip to the only local store open on Sundays, the Walmart in Ash Flat, was relatively uneventful. Samantha wished she'd thought to change into flat shoes before going shopping but all in all, she managed well.

"How about grabbing lunch?" John asked as they loaded their purchases into the open bed of his pickup truck. "The pizza place across the street used to be pretty good."

She hesitated. Yes, she was hungry. And tired. And stressed from the eventful morning. Yet she wasn't sure she was up to sitting in a familiar restaurant and sharing a meal with him. It might seem too much like one of their old dates, even though it wasn't, and she was afraid her blissful memories would be more than she could take right now.

"I should get home to Brutus. He's all alone."

"And armed to the *teeth,* pun intended. Besides, what are you going to do with him tomorrow when you have to go back to work? He'll be by himself then."

"I know. And I don't like it." Another problem suddenly occurred to her. "Uh-oh."

"What?"

"Will I have any way to get to work by then?"

"Probably not. I can pick you up. What time?"

She stopped tying the handles of the plastic grocery sacks long enough to make a face at him. "You don't think I'll have my car back by then?"

"I doubt it. Besides, how are you planning to drive it without keys or a decent place to sit?"

"You don't need to bother," she said with conviction. "I can phone a friend for a ride to work now that I have a new phone."

"Only if you can get it activated right away."

He was staring at her as if he could look through her eyes and see into the deepest reaches of her heart and mind.

That obvious emotional connection bothered Sam so much that she purposely averted her gaze. "You're a bundle of sunshine, aren't you? Why does everything have to be so complicated when you're concerned? I'm sure I can manage to activate a phone." The sound of his soft chuckle caused her to look up. "Well, I can."

Catching herself smiling, she realized she truly was glad to be in this man's company. What would it hurt to allow him to help her out for a day or so more? After all, they had been close at one time.

"Okay," Samantha said. "You win. I'll make us lunch back at the house and then you can listen while I talk to somebody in Outer Mongolia about transferring the old number to this new phone. That should be worth a couple of good laughs."

"At least. Here, let me tie the tops of those last bags for you."

"Fine. While you load them I'll go stow the cart in the rack. Be right back."

The afternoon sun warmed her face, lifted her spirits and put a spring in her step. The more she anticipated spending additional time with John, the more joy bubbled up, although she tried her best to tamp it down.

Shoving the shopping cart into the narrow storage area one row over from where he had parked, she turned and checked traffic to make certain it was safe to cross the lanes again.

It had never occurred to her that leaving John for mere moments might be hazardous until she heard the squeal of spinning tires and caught a glimpse of a beat-up, maroon-colored car racing toward her.

Sun glinted off its windshield and obscured the driver's face but she could see a man's beefy fists clenching the wheel. This was no potential accident. She was being attacked!

Jumping between the nearest parked cars Samantha closed her eyes and crossed her forearms in front of her face. Melding with her scream was the clenching, grinding sound of metal against metal and the shattering of breaking glass.

The car next to her was being shoved closer! She lost her balance as she turned to flee. The side of her head clipped an outside mirror on one of the sliding parked cars and she stumbled. Fell. The asphalt was hard and unforgiving.

Flashes of blinding light filled her closed eyes. Colors danced, flickered like a desert mirage.

An instant later the rippling, hazy edges of the picture converged, all the lights went out and she dropped into the welcome blackness of unconsciousness.

John had seen what was about to happen but was in the wrong position to intervene in time. He started to draw his weapon, then realized there was no way to be certain this was anything more than a driver's stupid mistake.

By the time the car that had been aimed at Samantha slewed into the next aisle and sped away, it was too late for him to take any aggressive action.

Instead, he raced toward the last place he'd seen her, vaulting over a wrinkled fender and landing nearby.

The sight of her, lying there so still, made his heart clench. If she hadn't stirred and moaned at that moment he didn't know what he'd have done.

Dropping onto his knees he pinned her shoulders. "Don't try to get up. You may be hurt. You shouldn't move."

"What?" Her eyes blinked rapidly, as if she was confused, then focused on him. "I'm okay. Really."

"Just the same, you should be checked over by a medic."

"I'm a nurse, John. I know when I'm injured. I'm fine. Honest. Let me up."

He reluctantly eased his hold, took her hands and helped her to her feet. "You sure?"

"Positive." She began to gently probe the side of her head with two fingers while scanning the parking lot. "I see the guy split. Did you get his license number?"

"No. He was moving too fast. I was more worried about you. What did you see?"

"Not much. Older car. Dirty. Probably rusty, too." Samantha rubbed her temple and winced. "Ouch. That smarts."

"I'm taking you to the E.R."

"Oh, no, you're not. I don't want to go there on a Sunday afternoon any more than you'd like spending your days off at the police station. If I start to get dizzy or have any other symptoms, I'll go see a doctor. I promise."

John cupped her elbow, urged her back to his truck and opened the passenger door as sirens wailed in the distance. "Fine. Sit right here where I can see you and behave yourself while

I give a statement to the Ash Flat cops. I'll try not to be gone long."

Pausing, he touched her hand. "Are you sure you're okay?"

"Positive."

The unshed tears dampening her long, dark lashes touched his heart. Sam might be so stubborn and self-assured that she drove him crazy, but there was still a vulnerability about her that made him sympathetic beyond common sense.

That's not the same thing as love, he insisted to himself, slamming the door and turning away. He was just feeling overly protective due to the calamities that had recently befallen her, that's all.

If that was true, then why had he had such a gut-level reaction to the thought that the speeding car might have injured her? he asked himself. And why was it such a struggle to merely walk a few yards away from her now? She'd be perfectly safe sitting in his truck.

Yeah, he countered, as safe as she'd been putting away their empty shopping cart.

He closed his eyes for a long moment and did what he knew he should have done immediately. He thanked God that Samantha had survived.

SIX

As Samantha waited for John to return she took further inventory of her injuries. All seemed slight except the bump on her head and since her vision was still good, she wasn't worried about concussion. Double-checking, she pulled down the visor and peered into the mirror so she could be certain the size of her pupils was equal.

That was when she saw the unexpected reflection in the background. Ben Southerland, his wife and son were leaving the store. They approached a car parked almost directly behind John's truck. Although they'd had to walk past the police cars and damaged vehicles, they hadn't seemed the least interested. Not that that was wrong. It just struck her as a bit unusual for a pillar of the community to pass by without stopping to offer aid.

"Oh, well," Samantha muttered, "this isn't the same as being in Serenity so he probably doesn't know those folks."

Curiosity kept her watching the little family. The boy was helped into the backseat of the silver-colored luxury sedan by his mother before she got in the front. Ben Southerland seemed to be the one doing all the talking and, judging by his body language, he was delivering a lecture.

Samantha had to slew in the seat to keep them in sight as they drove away. Bending her knee to do so pointed out another minor scrape. All she gave the injury was a cursory glance. She had other things on her mind.

The Southerland vehicle never got out of sight so she was positive it had pulled across the highway and entered the lot for the pizza restaurant. The same place John had offered to take her to lunch.

Should she tell him? Go there, too? No. Yes. Oh, rats. What real choice did she have? She'd been praying for a chance to observe the whole family and the Lord had just provided it. If she held to her previous plans and went home—where she'd already be if not for the delay caused by the collision—she would miss the opportunity to catch Ben Southerland interacting with his son.

Still, was she up to spending the next hour or so staring across one of those familiar booths at the man she had once dreamed of marrying?

"Yes. For Danny's sake," Samantha muttered.

"What?" a male voice asked.

Her head whipped around so fast she felt a wave of dizziness, proving she was not as totally unscathed as she'd claimed. "Hi, John. I guess I was talking to myself."

"So I'd gathered. Were you answering, too?" he asked, sliding behind the wheel and slipping his key into the ignition.

"Probably." Samantha gestured at the accident scene. "All through?"

"For now. I told them you said you weren't injured but gave them your name for the record. They know where to find us if they need anything else."

"In that case, I've decided to take you up on your offer of pizza, if that's okay."

"What made you change your mind?" He arched a brow at her. "The truth."

"I never intended to tell you anything but," Sam insisted. "While I was sitting here waiting for you I happened to notice the Southerlands going into that place across the highway. I just thought…"

"I get it. You won't have lunch with me unless there's a better reason than just enjoying a meal with an old friend."

"I'd hardly put it that way," she countered, realizing that her change of heart could look suspicious from his point of view. Little did he know how much effort she'd had to put into her decision. Unfortunately, she could hardly tell him she'd been resisting because she was afraid she'd enjoy his company more than she wanted to.

"Okay. Whatever you say." He dropped the truck into gear and backed out. "Fasten your seat belt."

Subdued by the fact that she'd hurt his feelings, Samantha followed directions. This was a no-win situation. If she confessed how deep, how poignant her memories were, he would know she'd been pretending that she no longer cared for him. If she let things stand as they were, he'd suffer needlessly.

One element of her dilemma stood out. If there was nothing left of her love for John Waltham, she would not be worried about whether or not he was upset. Therefore, the trick was going to be smoothing things over between them without letting him know her true sentiments. Since he had claimed he was able to read her like the proverbial book, she wondered if she was going to be able to pull it off.

One quick, sidelong glance at him insisted she must try. There was more than simple ire in his expression. The man was putting on an angry front but beneath his hard-hearted facade lay a tender heart; a heart that had been wounded by her unexplained choices.

Deciding to tell him enough to hopefully lift his spirits, she reached to touch his hand.

John abruptly pulled it away. "You don't have to pretend you like me, Sam. I'll help you, anyway."

"I wasn't…"

"Enough," he ordered.

He expertly maneuvered the truck across the highway and into the parking lot for the pizzeria. Without another word he got out, circled and opened her door for her.

Her scraped knee smarted when she slid to the ground but she hid the pain. There had been very few times in the past when John had gotten really mad at her. Back then, the only thing that had brought him around was having a chance to brood.

So, she let him escort her into the small, colorful restaurant without comment, chose a booth behind the Southerland family and settled in as if nothing was amiss.

Later, when John had had time to calm down she'd try again to explain. Probably. Maybe. Well, maybe not. If it looked as if he'd forgiven her later, there might be no need to hash it out.

That was her fondest hope. One she chose

to silently pray for while they waited for their order to be delivered.

"Which one is he?" John whispered behind his hand.

Samantha leaned closer across the tabletop and mouthed, "Over my shoulder," while also signaling by diverting her glance.

"Got it."

The man seated with his back to them looked innocuous enough. Middle-aged, neat brown hair, still clad in the slacks, vest, shirt and tie from the suit he'd probably worn to church.

The child wasn't visible over the high back of the booth bench but John could tell by the way the father was moving and speaking that the boy had to be beside him.

Moreover, the mother's eyes kept darting from her husband to her son as if she were concerned. John could tell there was plenty of tension in the family.

"Sit up straight," Southerland ordered, then added, "both of you."

That command caused Sam to stiffen her shoulders. John could understand why. If the tone hadn't been strident it might not have been so bad but there was a definite warning in the man's voice. He was unmistakably the boss.

"See?" Samantha asked, rolling her eyes.

"That's still not conclusive," John replied, his own voice casual. "Ah, here's our pizza. I hope you're hungry."

"Not really."

"Well, it smells delicious. You have to eat—unless there's something wrong that you've been keeping from me. How's your head?"

"It's fine."

"Then dig in." He loaded a plate with a slice of hot pizza and passed it to her. "I'm famished."

He knew he'd spoken a little too loudly due to the fact that his cop's instincts had kicked in. He'd have sworn under oath that the man sitting directly behind Sam had flinched when he'd asked about her head. Why? Was it because he'd recognized her voice? Or had he noticed them when they'd walked in and realized she was the E.R. nurse who had reported him?

Either was possible, but that didn't fully explain such a telling reaction. It looked as though Samantha might be right. Southerland might very well have something to hide. Something like the fact that he'd been abusing his son. No wonder she'd pegged him so easily. Even without prior knowledge of little Danny's injuries, John knew he would have been suspicious. The man's demeanor fairly screamed "watch me."

And he was going to, whether or not his boss—or Sam's—approved. Sometimes a cop just had to go with his gut instincts. This was one of those times.

Samantha managed to choke down two slices of pizza before her body insisted she stop. There hadn't been a lot to hear from the family seated behind her other than the usual comments about table manners and such. That, alone, was telling. Most parents at least conversed with each other, yet the Southerlands had been almost completely silent for the duration of the meal.

She noticed John's attention wavering and caught his eye. "What?"

"They're leaving," he said quietly. "And you should have seen the dirty look that guy gave you when he got up to go."

"So, he knew it was me sitting here. No wonder he was so quiet."

"Oh, he knew, all right. At least he did by the time he left. We have to assume he'd spotted us earlier."

"Do you think that's why he didn't talk much?"

"Maybe. Judging by his wife's reactions and the way she stuck so close to Danny on the way out, Mr. S has a rotten temper."

"I already told you that."

"Yeah. If I had any doubts before, I don't now. I just can't see what either of us can do about it."

"Now that Danny is on record for suspected abuse the only thing that might bring it to court is further injuries, and I hate to think of that happening." She shook her head as she met John's empathetic gaze. "I feel so helpless."

"Well, don't give up. You'll think of some way to intervene. What about CASA? Is there any way you might get yourself appointed as his spokesperson?"

"Only if I keep my distance. The rules say a volunteer advocate can't have any personal connection to the child's family. Now that I think about it, it's just as well we didn't make it to church this morning. Being part of the same congregation might disqualify me."

"Wait a minute. What about your E.R. work? You saw Danny then."

"Yes, but only in a professional capacity. If he had been treated by another nurse it would still be my job to interview her or him and make a record of medical observations for the judge. I think it's okay that I assisted the doctor when he treated Danny."

"Okay." John leaned back and stifled a yawn. "Sorry. I guess the adrenaline is wearing off."

"Mine, too. Shall we go? I don't want Brutus to think I've deserted him."

"You worry more about that dog than most folks do about people."

"He's my only family these days," Samantha said with a wistful smile.

"That's sad."

Her smile spread. "Oh, no. I love it this way. Brutus is always there, always glad to see me and he never loses his temper and snaps at me. I couldn't ask for a better companion."

"He's not much on conversation," John quipped as he rose and placed a tip on the table.

"No, but he watches the evening news with me when I'm working the day shift, like I am this coming week."

"That must be a barrel of laughs."

"Actually, he likes shows about animals the best. We watch a lot of those, too."

She saw John shaking his head as if he were criticizing her but the sparkle in his eyes and the quirking of one corner of his mouth told her otherwise.

Standing back as he paid at the cash register, Samantha was seized by a sense of déjà vu. How many other times had they shared a meal in this same pizzeria? How many times had they laughed over silly things and thoroughly enjoyed each other's company? How many times had they spent afternoons sitting in Elvina's porch swing and dreaming of a future together?

Too many, Sam concluded. She set her jaw, determined to choke back the emotions that were trying to take control. This was the very reason she'd hesitated to agree to eat here. This was what she'd feared. Remembering. Feeling as if they were the same as they had been five years ago. Wishing that nothing had changed.

But it had. Their past relationship was ancient history. Once John quit hanging around so much she'd be fine. Just peachy.

Turning away and starting for the exit so he couldn't see her face or tell she was distressed, Samantha sniffled quietly. She should have dug out an old purse and at least stuffed some tissues inside, even if she didn't have much else to put into it. Her credit cards had been canceled by phone but it would be tomorrow before she could see about getting a replacement driver's license and stopping payment on any blank checks that had been stolen.

One glance into the bed of John's pickup told her that at least their groceries hadn't been pilfered while they were inside eating. That was something, anyway. In a rural area like this such thefts were rare, yet judging by the way the past few days had been going for her, anything was possible.

Anything except letting herself forget that John Waltham was part of her history, not her present, she added, chagrined. For a few lovely moments during lunch, she'd let herself daydream and remember the good times, the special feelings that only he had ever brought to her heart and mind.

"Stupid, stupid, stupid," she muttered to herself as she climbed into the passenger side of the truck and slammed the door while he circled around front. "I never learn, do I?"

There was no valid rebuttal to that statement. Her only hope, if she could call it that, was to persevere until he got tired of hanging around and either solved the crime surrounding Bobby Joe's drug involvement or found a replacement to look in on her every so often.

When John joined her and started the engine without comment, Sam barely glanced in his direction. She didn't dare. She was afraid if he demonstrated even the smallest kindness, she might break down and weep for the potential happiness that had slipped through their fingers and trickled away like a handful of raindrops. Or tears.

The child cowered in the backseat of the moving car. He knew he'd better stay very still when his father was in a bad mood. Lately, that was all the time, especially when he'd been working too hard and came home after dark.

His mama always cried a lot then. Danny had heard their arguments from his room and had pulled the covers over his head to drown them out.

Sometimes, his mama came to his bedside and sat there for a while afterward, whispering to him while he pretended he was asleep.

When he got big and strong like his daddy he'd take care of her, he vowed. She wouldn't have to cry and be afraid then. They'd run away and find a nice house to live in with lots of pets and stuff like that.

The car slowed, then stopped. Danny heard the door slam so he peeked out. His daddy was standing at the curb talking to some men. They were all yelling and waving their arms.

"Mama?"

"Hush, honey. Be patient. Your father has some business to finish and then we'll go on home."

Danny drew up his knees, wrapped his thin arms around them and lowered his head so he wouldn't have to look. Being grown-up was scary. He hoped he'd be happier than his daddy was when he got to be a man.

SEVEN

Sam had allowed John to pick her up for work early the following morning but she'd asked Alice to give her a ride into town on their lunch break so she could apply for a replacement driver's license.

Since the sheriff's office and police headquarters were practically next door to the DMV, she was afraid she might accidentally run into John. When that didn't happen, she was actually disappointed.

"Proving once and for all that I am nuts," she mumbled, climbing back into Alice's two-door compact.

The older woman giggled. "You don't have to try to convince me. I know you."

"Thanks. Everybody needs friends who understand them."

"So, did you get the new license?"

"Uh-huh. It was easier than I'd thought. They

just took another picture, laminated a copy and that was that."

"Too bad it's not that easy to get your credit cards back."

"I went ahead and permanently canceled all but one of them. I don't live above my means so I really don't need credit except in emergencies."

"Speaking of emergencies, did you notice who showed up again today while you were on your morning coffee break?"

"No. Who? Not that I want to gossip," Samantha added.

"Oh, you'll be interested in this case. Remember that kid you were sure was being abused? Danny Southerland?"

"Yes…"

"Well, he came back. His mother brought him this time."

Sam's pounding heart sat like a lump in her throat. "How bad?"

"Bad enough, I guess." Alice gave a shake of her tight blond curls. "Weiss admitted him for observation."

"Oh, no. Why didn't somebody tell me?"

"I just did. And now that I see your face, I know who turned the case in to the cops the last time."

"How about this time? Was it reported?"

The other woman shrugged. "Don't know. I doubt it, although Dr. Weiss did seem a tad upset."

"I shouldn't wonder. Poor Danny."

"What are you going to do?"

"Make another report as soon as I've read the file and made sure this was no accident, I suppose. I saw the family just yesterday in Ash Flat. They all seemed pretty uptight, even then."

"I sure don't envy you when Weiss finds out you interfered," Alice said flatly. "You know how he feels about Ben Southerland. You could lose your job over it."

"I'll do the right thing and leave the fallout to the Lord the way I always do," Samantha replied. "If I let this situation go and something worse happens to that little boy, I'll never forgive myself."

The sight of Samantha crossing the Serenity square on foot hadn't surprised John nearly as much as he'd thought it would. Clearly, she'd followed through with her former notion and had asked someone from work to give her a lift into town from the hospital. That made perfect sense. He just felt let down—and pretty ridiculous, if he were honest with himself. After all, he and Sam were no longer a couple. Not even close. So why were his emotions lingering so close to the surface?

Deciding to act on a whim instead of heeding his personal misgivings, he sought out Levi Kelso and found him in his small, private office. "Are we done with the Rochard car, Chief?"

"I think so. Harlan had Adelaide dust it for prints but everything was pretty smudged. I don't think she got anything usable."

"We can release it, then? I thought I'd see about returning it."

"Fine, if you don't mind sitting on a pile of shredded foam."

"Maybe I'll call around and see if I can find a couple of decent replacement seats first. Is that fella who collected wrecks still out on Highway 9?"

"Naw. He gave up fixing old cars and went into the metal-recycling business years ago."

"Well, I can at least try to repair the driver's area so Samantha—I mean Ms. Rochard—can use her car."

The chief made a sound halfway between a snicker and a snort. "Might as well call her Samantha. Everybody else does. You're trying so hard to make us believe you're not interested in her, it's comical. Man up and admit it. You still have a thing for her."

"She's an old friend. That's all."

"Okay, have it your way. Walt can follow you out to the Rochard place and bring you back."

"Actually," John said, checking the time, "I thought I'd wait till Sam gets off duty, pick her up at the hospital then bring her by here so she can drive her car home herself."

"And that way you can tail her?"

John nodded soberly. "Yes. I have a bad feeling this whole mess is far from over."

"Okay. Suit yourself. There's a roll of duct tape in the storage closet. You can use that for patching. Adelaide mentioned that those seats looked even worse than she'd thought when she'd gone over the car for evidence. Must be pretty bad."

"They are. Thanks. I'll be out back if you need me."

His mind still focused on Samantha, John got the tape and headed for the parking area where the tow truck had left Sam's old sedan. When he opened the driver's door and looked inside, his jaw dropped.

Adelaide was right. This wasn't the way the car had looked when it had been towed into town. Now, the rip in the front seat far outdid the damage to the rear one, meaning that somebody had completed a thorough search while the car was parked right there behind the sheriff's department and Serenity police headquarters!

Turning on his heel John hurried back inside. "Chief! We need to dust the Rochard car again. Right now."

"Why?" Kelso rose slowly, both hands on his desk, and leaned forward, scowling. "What's going on?"

"The seats do look worse than before. Somebody's been at them again."

"You're joking."

John shook his head. "I'm totally serious. I know what that car looked like when I left it and it's nothing like what's out there now. Trust me. Whoever was searching it wasn't done. They finished their job in our parking lot."

Chief Kelso muttered under his breath. He was not only angry, he was embarrassed to have had more vandalism occur right under his nose. "All right. Grab an evidence kit and we'll go over the car ourselves before anything else happens to it. You can impress me with some of that expertise you picked up in Dallas."

"Yes, sir."

While the chief paused to let their dispatcher know where he was going, John pulled a fingerprint kit. His thoughts kept going back to Sam, to how she would react when he told her there had been a further search of her car. He was not looking forward to explaining how that could have happened or why they didn't have a real impound yard that was closed to outsiders the way larger departments did.

Behind him, Levi suddenly blurted out, "Fire!"

John whirled. Looked for the source within the office. That's when he saw his chief pointing at the back door and starting to run toward it while shouting, "Somebody call the fire department!" and grabbing a fistful of keys off pegs by the rear door.

Billows of black smoke were visible. John followed on his boss's heels, caught the heavy glass door before it had time to swing closed and raced outside.

Levi tossed him a key ring, pointed and bellowed, "Get that other patrol car moved farther away before we lose it, too. I'll take this one."

As John slid behind the wheel of one of the black-and-whites, he could see the formerly smoky aura becoming bright, dancing flames. Considering the fuel provided by the loose seat stuffing, it didn't matter how fast the fire department responded. There was no way any effort was going to save what was left of Sam's car now.

One quick call to Children's Services was all it took for Samantha to receive permission to interview Danny Southerland while he was still in the hospital. According to the social worker,

Brenda Connors, Sam's appointment via CASA had been approved. She was good to go. And just in time, because she wasn't about to let that poor kid leave the premises until she'd talked to him.

Seven-year-old Danny was asleep when Samantha entered his hospital room. The Serenity Medical Center didn't have a dedicated pediatric ward because the facility was too small, but there were several rooms that had been decorated with murals featuring cartoonlike animals painted in bright colors. Not only did children enjoy them, those rooms could be good for a laugh if an adult ended up housed there due to overcrowding.

The childish decor usually made Samantha smile but not this time. Seeing Danny looking so forlorn, so alone, lying on those stark-white sheets almost brought tears to her eyes. Her soft-soled shoes made no sound as she crossed to his bedside.

His tousled, reddish hair begged to be smoothed off his forehead. Her touch was gentle and light. His skin felt warm but not overly so.

Danny's eyelids fluttered as if he were dreaming. He began to whimper.

"Hush," Samantha crooned. "It's okay. You're safe."

Suddenly, the child gave a start and gasped.

His eyes flew open and he began to blink rapidly as if trying to get his bearings, and failing.

Samantha smiled at him. "You're okay, Danny. It's just me, Nurse Samantha. Remember me?"

Instead of answering, the boy levered himself onto an elbow and tried to peer past her.

Sam stepped aside. "It's just you and me, honey. There's nobody else here. See?"

As he relaxed back onto the pillows she took his wrist and checked his pulse. His little heart was hammering. "I'm sorry if I scared you, Danny. I just wanted to see how you were feeling."

He stared, wide-eyed and mute.

"You can talk to me if you want to. I'm your friend. Nurses and doctors help people when they're sick or hurt." She had thought she was getting through to him until she added, "Just like policemen do."

As soon as those last words were out of her mouth she rued them. Fresh fright replaced the confusion in the child's expression. He withdrew, gathered up the top border of the sheet that covered him and once again began staring at the open door.

Samantha let down one of the side railings so she could perch lightly on the edge of the bed and affect a calming posture while she explained. "You don't need to be afraid of anybody or anything while you're here with us, Danny. Do you understand?"

Thankfully, she saw a barely discernible nod so she continued. "Good. I want to help you. Besides being a nurse, I sometimes help kids who need me for other reasons." Pausing, she tenderly touched his hand. This was a perfect opportunity to learn more about his home life without asking directly so she said, "You can think of me as your extra mama."

Danny blinked rapidly, studying her face as if struggling to believe her. The most telling aspect of his glance was the fact that he'd shown no additional fear when she'd mentioned his mother.

"Where's my mama?" came out so quietly Sam might have missed it if she hadn't been watching his lips move.

"She's not here now, but I'm sure she'll come to visit you later." Sam counted to ten silently. "I imagine your daddy will come, too."

The unspoken proof she'd been seeking appeared instantly. Danny not only cringed at the mention of his father, he pulled the sheet higher and tucked it beneath his chin as if it were a shield.

Samantha gathered herself, as well. It would be counterproductive to let any anger toward his parents show. She knew that. She also knew that if Ben Southerland had been standing there at that moment, she might have given him a piece of her mind. Of course she didn't dare break protocol that way. An emotional outburst could cost her this CASA assignment and perhaps also disqualify her from others in the future.

Therefore, she took a deep, settling breath and forced a smile for the boy's sake. "Tell you what, Danny. I'm about to go get myself an ice cream bar. Would you like me to bring you one?"

His eyes never left the empty doorway and she could tell he was visualizing his father there so she rose and blocked his view. His medical records had already told her his injuries were minor and that he was ambulatory, so she held out her hand.

"How about coming with me to get the ice creams? I'll help you put on a robe and slippers if you want."

"Okay…"

The reply was softly spoken yet clearly a positive sign. Since Dr. Weiss was still out to lunch, he wouldn't be checking on Danny for a while longer and, truth to tell, she didn't see why the boy had been admitted in the first place—unless Weiss had finally seen the light and started to believe his so-called buddy had been abusing his son, as Alice had inferred. There was always that hope.

With Danny's hand grasping hers and his trust growing, she led him quietly out of the room and down the hallway to the vending-machine niche. A little ice cream wouldn't hurt him and sharing a treat would help strengthen their emotional bond.

This was the first step toward learning the truth from a child who was too frightened of further abuse to speak honestly. It was hard to listen without comment when children finally opened up to her, but it was also a blessing to be there for them.

She was their literal guide to health and well-being. It was her recommendations to a judge that could save innocent lives and set these kinds of youngsters on the path to normalcy. Any personal angst, any depth of emotional suffering, was worth it to Samantha if the end result was a happy little boy or girl.

One who was no longer afraid.

The ice cream adventure completed, she had escorted Danny back to bed and left him there after showing him how to find the cartoon channel on the television.

John was entering through the E.R. door when she returned to her regular post. Judging by his determined expression, he was on a mission.

Sam assumed he had come to see her. She

started to smile in greeting, then noticed how morose he seemed. "Hi. What's up? You look terrible."

"I feel terrible," he said, taking her arm and guiding her off to the side of the room. "It's about your car."

"I thought you might have come to tell me you were done with it. Guess not, huh?"

"Oh, we're done with it, all right. Only not for the reasons I wish."

Studying his face and scowling, Sam was struck by how much he seemed to be struggling. Surely he wasn't still blaming himself for not watching her house more closely.

"Well, are you going to tell me or make me drag it out of you? What's wrong?"

"Somebody set your car on fire while it was parked behind the station. It's a total loss."

"*What?* How can that be?"

"Let's sit down and talk, Sam."

"I don't need to sit anywhere. Just spit it out. What's going on? What happened?"

"Okay." He shrugged. "We know the car was searched again, for starters. Apparently, whoever was responsible decided to burn it to remove any possible traces of their identity."

"In broad daylight? In downtown Serenity? Surely somebody saw something."

"Not as far as we can tell. We've canvassed

the nearby businesses. Nobody noticed anything odd—until we saw the smoke."

"You called the fire department?"

John grimaced. "Of course. By the time they arrived there was no saving the car. I spoke to one of the firefighters who knows you. Mitch Andrews?"

"Right. He and Jill are adopting the Pearson orphans. I told you about helping them when we were talking about my CASA cases. Which reminds me…"

John interrupted. "Yeah, that's what Mitch said, too. He told me it was obvious there was accelerant poured into the car. Once it was lit, nothing could have put it out. I'm sorry."

"You're *sorry?* I'm devastated. Now what will I do for wheels?"

"What about the old barge Elvina used to drive? I thought I noticed it parked in your barn."

"That thing hasn't been started in years. I imagine the mice have eaten all the wiring."

"I'll check it for you tonight."

"Tonight?" She could tell he was highly stressed. His posture was stiff and his demeanor uneasy. "You look as if you're cooking up some kind of devious plan and you're afraid I won't like it."

"You probably *aren't* going to like it. That

can't be helped. Levi, Harlan and I have talked the situation over and they're going to loan me the little travel trailer they use once in a while for an on-site operations headquarters. I'll tow it out to your farm tonight when I drive you home and camp there."

"You will not."

"I told them you'd pitch a fit but they were both firm about it. Harlan says he can't spare Adelaide, and Levi doesn't want me sleeping in my car and losing my edge, so they worked out a way where I'll be handy most of the time you're home. There's no other choice—unless you intend to invite me in and consider me a houseguest."

"I could refuse to be watched at all," she said, realizing almost immediately that that was not going to suit anyone, herself included. She had been frightened out of her wits lately, more than once, and was not looking forward to spending dark, spooky nights alone so far out in the country.

The way she saw the situation, she'd have to allow someone to stay close by in order to feel safe. Since she knew John better than any of the other deputies or police officers, assigning him to the job did make perfect sense.

Samantha could tell he was searching her expression, waiting for her to capitulate once logic kicked in.

"All right," she finally said, letting herself begin to smile as she formulated her full reply. "I'll let you camp on my property, but only because I don't want anything bad to happen to Brutus, and you and he are buddies."

"Right." The shadow of humor twitched at the corner of John's mouth. "For Brutus."

"Yes. That way, if you end up prowling around outside, he won't attack you and you won't get scared and accidentally shoot him. It's a great plan."

"Okay. Do you have any preference as to where I park?"

"I guess not. If you pull straight through the carport you can disconnect there, although you'll have to check that the crossbeams are high enough to miss the vents on the top of the trailer."

"You want me that close?" He was beginning to smile and look terribly confident.

"Well, you won't be much use to me parked way out in the field or stuck inside the barn," Samantha said, certain she sounded reasonable rather than overly eager.

When John's grin spread she added, "Just don't get the idea that having you there will make me careless. I fully intend to bolt my doors."

"Good. Are those new locks I installed working okay for you?"

"Fine, although I don't know how much use they'd bc if some really big guy decided he wanted to kick the door in."

"Which is exactly why the chief assigned me to stay at your place temporarily," John countered. "I'm glad you approve."

She was about to amend his statement when he laughed softly and added, "For Brutus's sake, of course."

EIGHT

John was already towing the small, white trailer when he returned to the medical center to pick up Samantha that evening, just after five. She came out the door and jogged toward him before he had a chance to park and go inside to fetch her.

He leaned across to open the truck's door but she was already climbing in. "Next time, wait for me to walk you out," he ordered.

"Don't be silly. I looked around first. There's nobody sinister lurking out here. Besides, it's always broad daylight when I get through with the day shift. I wouldn't have been out here so late a few nights ago if I hadn't been subbing for a nurse who had a family emergency."

"Yeah, well, day or night, we didn't see anyone in the store parking lot in Ash Flat when you were almost run over, either. Next time, wait for me, Sam. Promise."

"Okay, okay. I will." Sobering, she fastened

her seat belt. "This is hard for me, you know. I've been totally independent for years. It feels funny having to ask for permission to do things."

"I don't mean it that way," John insisted.

"Then what *do* you mean?" She waved her hands rapidly as if to erase her statement. "Oh, never mind. I get the general idea. So, have you made any progress with Bobby Joe's case?"

"No. But I did mention your interest in Ben Southerland when I was talking to the chief. He says the guy is squeaky-clean."

"Hah! Then why is Danny in the hospital?"

John's grip tightened on the steering wheel and his head whipped around. *"What?* Is he okay?"

"Yes. More bruises, mostly. I started to fill you in earlier but after you told me about my car burning up it totally slipped my mind."

"Did you report abuse again?"

"Sure did. I called Child Protective Services. And this time the right authorities listened."

"Good. What about the boy's safety? Are they going to take him away from his parents?"

"I don't know. He's safe enough while he's still with us. The doctor has promised to delay his release until a judge has heard the case."

"Is that enough?"

"It's a start," Samantha said. "I have other

good news, too. I've been assigned as Danny's official CASA representative. That means I'll be able to intervene to help him. And it will also give me access to any other records there may be from the past."

"Hmm. The Southerlands can't have always lived here or I'd know them. Where are they from?"

"Georgia, I think. At least that's their most recent former address. If I find out they've moved around a lot it will be an even bigger red flag."

"Because they might have a record of abusing Danny in other states?"

"Yes." She pressed her lips into a thin line and shook her head. "It's a good thing for his father that I'm a woman. If I were a man I might be tempted to give him a taste of the punishment his son has had to endure."

"No, you wouldn't," John said tenderly. "But I do understand how you feel. There were plenty of times when I wanted to do that to your dad."

Had he spoken too boldly? John wondered. Revealing the unvarnished truth was not always wise, especially since he wasn't positive how Sam was currently relating to her parents.

When she turned her face to him, however, and softly said, "Thank you," he knew it was going to be all right.

"You went through a lot back in those days. I wish I could have done more for you."

"You were my friend. You stood by me when I wanted to move in with Elvina, and my folks pitched a fit. That was plenty."

"But they still needled you about coming back to live with them, especially until you were out of high school." Pausing, he wondered if it was necessary to say more, to tell her that his efforts to get her to leave Serenity with him had been an attempt to distance her more from her familial trials.

"Yes, they did," Sam said, "but by that time, Elvina and I had grown very close. Once I'd experienced life under her roof, it felt as if I was living with my real grandmother."

"It still would have been easier on you if you'd married me and let me take you away from here," John said with a brief but telling sigh.

Samantha shook her head. "No. It would have been idiotic. You'd have eventually realized that in trying to rescue me you'd imprisoned yourself—for life. I couldn't let you make that kind of sacrifice, John. I know you meant well, but neither of us was ready for marriage."

No mention of love or the blissful contentment he'd expected them to find together, he noted. And not a single indication she'd understood a word he'd said when he'd tried to explain how he'd felt, then or now. It was as if they had each participated in the same encounters, the same conversations, yet had viewed them in a completely different light.

That was how it often was with eyewitnesses to a tragedy or a heinous crime, he reminded himself. A person related an incident based on what their personal background happened to be, which was why such reports were often so contradictory.

He and Sam had done the same thing with respect to their past. He had seen them as being madly in love and she had seen only that he was trying to liberate her. Her view was correct, as far as it went. What she had missed was the deep, unconditional way he had loved her.

The way, if he allowed himself to admit it, he still did.

Gaze searching the passing countryside, Samantha had to stop herself from actually holding her breath. It was almost as if she were standing outside during a thunderstorm and waiting for a bolt of lightning to strike right at her feet. Thankfully, they were almost home and nothing else strange or threatening had happened. Yet.

"You okay?" John asked.

She wished he wouldn't stare at her that way.

It would be a lot easier to reassure him that she was fine if she didn't have to do it to his face. *Not that a positive response would be a lie,* she reasoned for the sake of her conscience. It was simply harder to say and do anything in a calm manner when he was sitting this close.

"I'm great," Sam finally replied. "I just want to get home, check on Brutus and chill with my best bud."

"Well, okay," John drawled, "but the dog won't like it if we don't include him."

"I *meant* the dog," Sam shot back, realizing belatedly that John had been baiting her and she'd fallen for one of his silly ruses exactly the way she used to.

She folded her arms across her chest and tried her best to work up a show of displeasure. That would have been a lot easier if she hadn't heard her companion start to chuckle softly.

Frowning and smiling at the same time, she glanced over at him. "You are hopeless, Waltham. You know that?"

"Yup. So you've told me often enough." He laughed a little more before sobering. "Seriously, Sam, we need to talk about a plan of defense so we're ready for anything."

"Like what?"

"Like keeping each other on speed dial and

making sure neither of us goes anywhere without informing the other."

"What you really mean is, you don't want me to make a move unless I tell you first. Right?"

"Well…"

"Then say it. I might as well be the one under arrest instead of Bobby Joe. I have very little more freedom than he does."

Instead of agreeing or arguing or reacting in any of the ways Samantha had expected, John merely nodded.

When he said, "Believe me, I'd prefer you were in jail where every cop in town could keep an eye on you," she felt the urge to deliver a scathing rebuttal.

Instead, she smiled sweetly and said, "I'm really sorry you got stuck babysitting me. I guess we'll just have to make the best of a bad situation and get through it as fast as possible. Right?"

"Right."

Sam noticed how firmly his hands were gripping the steering wheel and saw his jaw muscles clenching. He was really uptight. Well, too bad. This police protection assignment hadn't been her idea in the first place. It wasn't her fault that he was stuck with her. And she certainly wasn't going to continue to apologize for their awkward situation when none of it was her doing.

John eased the truck and trailer into her driveway and started to slowly approach the house while Samantha sat there and fumed. Okay, so he didn't want to be with her and had made no bones about his feelings. She could take that. It wasn't the first time she'd been rejected and it certainly wouldn't be the last.

But, in the back of her mind, she'd hoped…

No, she insisted, steeling herself for whatever was to come. She would not start wishing for things that were beyond impossible. She'd learned the hard way that that was futile. John Waltham was only there beside her, protecting her, because he'd been ordered to. And he would do his job to the best of his ability, as always.

Samantha could understand that kind of work ethic because she possessed the same kind of dedication. That was why she'd laid her job on the line, more than once, in an effort to help the helpless. And it was why she would do the same thing again, in a heartbeat, if she suspected any child was in jeopardy.

Picturing Danny and remembering his fright, she momentarily closed her eyes and shot a quick prayer heavenward. "Father, be with him. Keep him safe," was all she deemed necessary. She was a no-nonsense person with regard to her daily existence and didn't stray far from that approach in other areas.

Perhaps that was one reason she'd gone into nursing, she concluded. She liked to see things done well and handled properly, efficiently. Having order in her life made up for the chaos of her childhood, for the moment-by-moment uncertainty, for the deep-seated fear that even now occasionally surfaced and caught her unawares.

Samantha shivered and wrapped her arms around herself to hold her nylon jacket tighter over her hospital-type scrubs. The iciness was more in her mind than her body. It kept company with unreasonable dread and the feeling that she might be on the receiving end of more senseless violence at any moment.

Lashes lowered, she chanced a sidelong glance at her companion. He wasn't paying the slightest attention to her. He didn't have to. Just seeing him there beside her was enough. As always, John Waltham's mere presence both blessed and comforted her.

John drove his rig around the farmhouse and carefully checked the trailer's clearance before easing it beneath Sam's carport. Thankfully, there was plenty of room.

While he was doing that, she jumped out and headed for the back door.

"Wait. I'll go in with you," he called. "Just let

me get unhitched so the truck isn't hampered by this extra weight."

"What difference does that make?"

She had paused with her hand on the doorknob and he could tell she wasn't likely to listen to anything but the most blunt warning.

"One, we may want to make a quick getaway and the trailer will slow us down. And two, I want to check the house before you go wandering around in it."

"Oh, please."

Seeing her rolling her eyes and knowing what she was liable to do next, he left his unhitching task half finished and joined her on the back porch, taking the steps two at a time.

She held up her new house key. "Here. I suppose you'll want this."

"Thanks." As John took the key, his hand brushed Samantha's and a tingle shot up his arm. Did she sense the same extent of awareness he did? A quick glance at her expression hinted that she might, yet there was no smile ticking at the corners of her mouth, no typical twinkle in her dark eyes.

He eased the key ring from her hand, letting his touch linger as long as he thought he dared, and fit the key into the shiny, brass lock. Something seemed off, although he couldn't quite put his finger on what it might be.

Scowling, he looked over his shoulder at Samantha. "Do you sense any problems?"

"No. Why?"

"I can't say. It just feels wrong, somehow."

"Probably because you're opening my door instead of yours. This whole stupid situation feels weird to me."

"No argument there," John said.

He turned the knob. The door swung open. The kitchen was dimly lit, the house was quiet. He froze. Turned to Sam. Saw her understanding dawn.

They had not been greeted. There was no sign of her old, faithful dog.

Samantha pushed past him. "Brutus! Where are you? Here, Brutus. Here, boy."

John grabbed her arm to stop her from going any farther. "No. Wait. Let me check first."

"Let go of me. He's my dog."

She tried to twist free but John held her fast. "And you want to be in good enough shape to take care of him if he needs you."

He pushed her back as he drew his gun and started from the kitchen into the hallway. "At least stay behind me."

Samantha gave his shoulders a hard push. "Then go. Hurry. He might be hurt."

Or worse, John thought, keeping that morbid notion to himself. If anything had happened to

Sam's dog she'd be inconsolable, and with good reason. She and Brutus had more than a long history together, they shared a difficult past that had forever tied them to each other.

Large-breed dogs like hers didn't usually live as long as smaller ones did and the old dog might have simply laid down and gone to sleep, never to awaken. That would be bad, yes, but not nearly as hard to take as if Brutus had been the victim of the criminals who had been targeting Sam.

Her voice weakening and starting to break, she kept calling, "Brutus, Brutus," as they made their way through the house and completed their inspection.

Back in the living room, John holstered his gun and turned to her. "I'm sorry, Sam. He's not here."

"He has to be. He was fine when I left him this morning. There were new locks on the doors and they haven't been broken or tampered with. I saw you check them. So how could he get out?"

"I don't know. Are you positive he didn't slip past you as you were leaving this morning?"

"You picked me up. Did you see him come outside?"

"No. And he's pretty hard to miss, especially since he usually stays so close to you."

"Then where is he?"

The sight of tears slipping past her dark lashes and starting to trickle down her cheeks hit John like a sucker punch. He opened his arms. She stepped into his embrace.

As he held her and she wept silently, his practiced glance kept sweeping that room and the part of the hallway he could see. There had to be a clue. Something that would lead them in the right direction. Why would a criminal bother the harmless old dog, yet leave the house intact?

Reluctant to ease his hold on Sam, he nonetheless took a step back so he could look into her eyes as he spoke. "I think we may have missed something, honey. We were looking for Brutus, not other clues."

He took her hand. "Come on. We're going to search this place again from top to bottom. And this time, I want you to look for anything that may be different. Understand?"

"Yes." She sniffled. "Like what?"

"Hopefully, we'll know it when we see it."

"You don't think he just wandered off?"

"No," John said flatly. "I suspect he either slipped out when someone opened the door or…"

"Or what?"

"Or, he's been dognapped."

NINE

Samantha couldn't believe her ears. "Dog-napped? But who? Why?"

"*Who* is the biggest question. If the dog knew the person who took him he probably went willingly. If he didn't, I think we'd better keep an eye out for signs that his kidnapper is suffering from a dog bite."

"You call the police. I'll call the hospital," Samantha said, eager to have something to do besides worry and weep. She hated any show of weakness and had thought she was too strong-willed to succumb to it—until her best friend had disappeared. Worse, she'd shed tears all over John's uniform shirt. What must he think of her?

Stepping aside, she took her cell phone from the pocket of her scrub top and called the E.R.

When she was done explaining the situation she looked to her companion. His expression was not encouraging.

"No one has come to the E.R. complaining of a dog bite. What did your chief say?"

"That he's not going to consider a lost dog as a crime. Unless we can come up with something else that gives him a better reason to investigate, we're on our own."

"Then let's go." She grabbed his hand to hurry him along.

"Wait. Stop and think. Since nobody jimmied the door locks we need to look more closely at the windows. You had them all latched, right?"

"Yes. I double-checked every one before I went to bed last night."

"Okay. Then the next order of business is for us to go over the yard and look for tracks."

"Brutus is out there all the time. His paw prints will be everywhere."

"It's impressions from strange boots or shoes we're looking for, especially if they happen to be next to the most recent tracks left by the dog. And while we're at it, keep an eye out for signs of injury—not to Brutus, to whoever took him."

"He still might have wandered off. He's been known to chase armadillos."

"It's been daylight from the time you left for work until now. Armadillos are nocturnal."

"I know. I just…" She knew if she kept talking her voice would falter so she quieted. This whole predicament seemed impossible. She had thought about someone trying to get at her by waging personal attacks but it had never occurred to her that anybody would be evil enough to take out their animosity on a defenseless animal like Brutus.

Why not? she immediately asked herself. People abused their own children all the time. What was to keep them from hurting a dog? She'd rescued Brutus from that very situation once and she'd do whatever it took to save him a second time.

If they could find him before it was too late.

John checked the interior of the dilapidated barn and found nothing, then slowly circled the house, his eyes on the ground, his hand grasping Samantha's so he'd be certain of exactly where she was every second.

Suddenly, she gave a yank.

He whirled, the heel of his free hand jumping to the butt of his holstered sidearm. "What? What do you see?"

"There." She was pointing up. "That ladder. It's usually in the barn. I've never needed it so I'm not positive it's the one I keep out there but it sure looks the same."

His chin lifted, his gaze settling on the second story. "Do you use the attic much?"

"No. I haven't been up there in years. Elvina and I emptied it long before she passed away."

"Well, somebody's been messing around up there," John said. He started for the base of the ladder, made sure it was well positioned, then put a boot on the bottom rung. "Stay here. I'll go check it out."

The obstinate look on Sam's face told him what her opinion was long before she opened her mouth to speak.

"No way, mister. If you're going up, I'm going up."

"You can steady the ladder for me."

"In a pig's eye."

"Sweet talk will get you nowhere, Ms. Rochard. We can either stand here arguing or you can back off and let me do my job. Your call."

"If I wasn't so worried about Brutus you know exactly what I'd do." Nevertheless she took several steps back, cleared the way for him and spread her arms wide. "All right. You win. Go ahead."

As John climbed toward the attic he remained on alert, ready for an attack. It didn't come. Instead, he found the small window smashed and the sash lifted. Broken glass littered the dust-covered attic floor. Footprints crossed the room and disappeared into a stairwell.

Once inside, he inspected the area carefully

with a flashlight, then leaned out to call down to Samantha. "There's nobody here now but it looks like there was." He waved his cell phone and flipped it open. "I'll report a B and E. Breaking and entering. That won't bring a fast response the way a robbery in progress would, but I want this incident on record just the same."

"What about Brutus? Is there any sign of him up there?"

John shook his head. "No. Nothing."

"Well, at least…"

He knew exactly what she was thinking even though she didn't finish putting it into words. At least the old dog's body wasn't lying up there. That meant there was still a chance he'd survived.

Was it wrong to pray for the safety of an animal? John didn't think so, but just to be on the safe side he focused his heavenly plea on Samantha's well-being and her need for the return of her faithful companion.

His "Amen" echoed as he crossed the attic, careful to avoid stepping in the prints he'd discovered, and started to descend the interior staircase into the main part of the house, inspecting the narrow passageway as he went.

When he slipped a handkerchief over the knob and opened the door at the base of the stairway, he was startled to find Sam standing there. "I told you to wait outside. What if there had been someone hiding on these stairs?"

"But there wasn't." Her eyes were wide, her expression a cross between persistence and pleading. "What did your chief say? Is help coming now?"

"Not code three, if that's what you're asking. Levi said to seal off the attic and he'd get somebody out here as soon as possible. Since the perp is gone and we didn't find anything missing, they're not considering it a robbery, or even a real crime scene, at least not yet."

"My *dog* is missing! I don't care about anything else. Doesn't anybody understand that?"

"I do," John said, reaching for her hand.

She pulled it away. "Then *do* something."

"What would you have me do, Sam? We've covered the whole house and the yard. Brutus is gone." Unshed tears had dampened her lashes again and were threatening to slip down her reddened cheeks.

"Everything started with Bobby Joe Boland," she said, sniffling. "I'm going to go make him tell me everything."

John watched her stalk off and wondered how long it would take her to realize she was afoot without him. It turned out to be about four seconds.

Samantha whirled. Waved her arms. "Well,

come on. Let's get that trailer unhitched and hit the road."

"What makes you think you'll be allowed to talk to a prisoner? The sheriff and Chief Kelso have rules, you know."

"And you're going to help me get around them," Sam said flatly. "One way or the other."

"Oh, yeah?"

He almost laughed aloud when she fisted her hands on her hips, stuck out her chin and simply said, "Yeah."

"Well, okay, then."

Keeping his face averted as he returned to the trailer and continued to disconnect it, John worked to hide his intense admiration. That woman had been resilient and continually surprising as a teen. As a mature adult she was a marvel. Or, as Elvina used to say, Sam was a real pistol; a cornered wildcat with a chip on her shoulder and the grit of a catfish caught on a trotline.

"You're laughing at me, aren't you?" Sam asked, sounding miffed.

John straightened. "No. I am definitely *not* laughing at you."

"Then what's with that stupid grin?"

"Let's just say I'm coming to fully appreciate your courage and perseverance."

"Well, don't give me too much credit," Samantha countered. "I am determined we'll find Brutus but I'm still scared to death we'll be too late."

If John had voiced his thoughts at that precise moment it would have meant agreeing with her, so he remained silent. They could not be too late. That was simply unacceptable.

Samantha was lost in the depths of her vivid imagination and struggling to sort her thoughts into usable form when her new cell phone played her a tune.

John looked across the truck's cab as he drove. "Aren't you going to answer that?"

She shook herself from her doldrums and pawed through the shoulder bag she'd picked up to replace the stolen one. "Oops. I didn't recognize that new music. Hello?"

Listening, her heart began to pound and her hand trembled. "Okay. I'll be right there."

"Is it Brutus?" John asked. "Did somebody find him?"

"No. The social worker I work with, Brenda Connors, wants me to meet her at the hospital ASAP. She just heard that Danny's father is trying to check him out against the doctor's orders."

"What can *you* do?"

"I don't know. Maybe talk him down or at

least stall long enough for Brenda to get there, too. Thankfully, we're only minutes away."

She eyed her companion's uniform. "Brenda said she called the police, but even they can't stop a parent from taking a child home unless there's been a court order preventing it. Maybe you can bluff him."

"Okay. Whatever you need."

"It might cause you trouble with your chief," she warned. "It's not technically legal."

"But it's the right thing to do." John smiled as he increased his speed. "As an old friend of mine likes to say, 'Do the right thing no matter what.'"

"Who? Me?" In spite of her anxiousness she appreciated the compliment. John did see her reasoning and understand her motives. That made him more than a friend, it made him a valuable ally. They were in a war for the well-being of children and every skirmish was one more step toward the ultimate goal of rescue. She knew she couldn't save them all but she was determined to do everything in her power to help those few kids whose lives touched hers.

All across the country, other volunteers were doing the same things, fighting the same kinds of battles and defending the innocents, one court date at a time.

Samantha clenched her jaw. If she let herself

think about all the children who had no advocates, no one to speak on their behalf, the burden was almost overwhelming.

Father, get us to the hospital in time to help Danny, she prayed silently. *Please, please, please!*

John chose the closest parking place and skidded to a stop. They both jumped out of the truck, hurrying toward the glassed front entrance.

"No black-and-whites yet," John remarked. "Looks like we beat the reinforcements."

"We don't have to wait for backup, do we?"

"No. Just let me go in first," he said, surprised to see her fall back at the door so he could pass. Apparently, she did have some sense when it came to self-preservation, although he sure hadn't seen much sign of it before now.

"I'll go check our computers to see if we've gotten a legal hold order yet," Sam said. Veering off toward the office area she called over her shoulder, "Danny's down the south hall, room one-ten. Meet you there in a few minutes."

"Got it."

John was just short of breaking into a run. Keeping his impatience under control wasn't easy. He shortened his strides, then slowed even more. One-oh-six, one-oh-eight… There it was. One-ten.

The door was closed but a thin, pale, young nurse was standing in the hallway, wringing her hands and looking upset enough that it caused him to hesitate and ask, "What's going on?"

"It's awful." She eyed his uniform, her frightened gaze lingering on his badge. "I'm so glad you're here. Dr. Weiss is arguing with a parent. He sent me out of the room and told me to call Social Services. When I came back they were yelling so loud I was afraid to interrupt."

"Okay. I'll take over. You go outside and wait for the other deputies so you can direct them to the right place."

"Yes, sir. Gladly."

John paused barely long enough for the panicky nurse to make herself scarce, then knocked. Without waiting for an invitation to enter, he pushed open the door and placed himself squarely in the doorway. "Evening, folks. Is there a problem?"

Ben Southerland turned from confronting Dr. Weiss, rounded on John and shook his fist. "Go away. We don't need the cops. There wouldn't be any problem if these bureaucrats would stop insisting on useless red tape. If they don't get their act together in the next few minutes I'm going to take my son and leave, with or without permission."

"I'm sure the hospital has the boy's best interests at heart," John said calmly.

"He's a minor. I'm his father. And if I say he's leaving with me, he's leaving with me." Pivoting, the man reached for Danny.

Instead of waiting meekly for capture, the child ducked, scooted beneath the covers then scrambled to the foot of the bed where there was a gap between the footboard and the side rail.

John saw him slide to the floor, then clamber under the bed and draw himself up into a ball, thin arms wrapped tightly around his bent, knobby knees.

Roaring displeasure, Southerland circled the bed and made a wild grab for the child.

Danny bolted.

John lunged and snagged him around the waist in passing. For a second he wondered if he'd tangled with a bobcat instead of a slightly built seven-year-old. The boy went wild, shrieking, kicking and thrashing so forcefully John was afraid he'd hurt himself, not to mention inflict damage on his erstwhile rescuer.

"Easy," John kept saying, but there was certainly nothing easy about containing this frantic child. Between the pummeling punishment of the small fists and feet and trying to keep Danny out of his father's grasp, John was rapidly running out of options.

Southerland shoved the doctor out of the way and made a grab for John's arm. "Let go of my son."

He dodged. "I will, as soon as everybody calms down."

That promise did nothing to placate either the man or the boy. Every new effort Ben made led to renewed attempts to escape and the terrified child began to wail.

John saw the irate father draw back his arm. He swiveled to shield Danny and took the full force of the blow to the side of his head near the temple. It staggered him. He faltered, loosening his hold.

Danny hit the floor running—and barreled right into Samantha's open arms.

Stunned but still conscious, John saw the tiled floor coming up to greet him. He caught himself on his hands and knees and shook his head to try to clear it. People were moving and shouting within his sphere of vision, yet their actions didn't seem to make sense. At least not enough to allow him to act.

Southerland bent over John and managed to wrest his sidearm from its holster. He straightened, casting about as if he were hardly aware of where he was or what he was doing.

Samantha saw a wildness in his eyes, blind futility coupled with the determination to escape no matter how high the cost.

He swung around and pointed the gun directly at her! Samantha pivoted to try to protect the little boy but she knew that any bullet fired from that short a distance could easily pass through her body and still wound the child, perhaps fatally.

She wanted to run but her feet stayed rooted to the floor. Danny clung to her and sobbed as if his little heart was breaking. So was hers. She just hoped she'd live long enough to see him permanently removed from the hazardous environment in which he had spent his early years.

All she could think to do was hold him tight and pray without words, reaching out to God as if He were a life preserver and she was drowning in a bottomless well.

Her pulse beat in her ears until it drowned out reality. Clinging to the child, she waited, wondering if this was going to be the instant she drew her final breath.

The room was spinning. Time stood still. Then, she realized she was hearing rapid footsteps echoing down the hallway and fading away.

She chanced a look. Danny's father was gone. And so was the doctor.

* * *

John recognized the voice calling his name. It was Samantha. And she sounded worried. If Southerland was unhinged enough to take a swing at a uniformed officer of the law, there was no telling what else he might do.

Leaning on the bedstead, John pulled himself up and blinked to clear his vision. Samantha was still standing by the open door with the child clinging to her. He reached to rest his palm on the butt of his sidearm, just in case—and found an empty holster!

That was enough of a shock to supply a jolt of head-clearing adrenaline. John tensed. Scanned the room. He and Sam were the only adults present.

"Where did everybody go?" John asked.

She shook her head and quickly came to his side. "I don't know. Ben looked as surprised as the rest of us were when you went down. Then he grabbed your gun and started waving it around. I was afraid he was going to shoot us all but he ran instead. I guess Dr. Weiss followed him."

Reassuring the child as she placed him back in bed, she studied John's pupils and gently cupped his cheek. "Look straight at me."

"I'm fine. He just blindsided me, that's all."

"You took the blow meant for someone else."

"It won't matter what excuse the guy decides to give for swinging. Assault on a cop will land him in jail." John reached for the radio clipped to his belt, reported the threat of an armed and dangerous suspect and gave Southerland's description. In the distance, sirens already wailed.

Samantha folded her arms across her chest and gave him a lopsided smile. "That went well, don't you think?"

"Yeah, great." He eyed the quivering child who had once again assumed the balled-up pose he'd struck while hiding under the bed. "Suppose you introduce me to Danny here and tell him I'm one of the good guys. I'd hate to have to go through another wrestling match with him. He is one tough kid."

"Gladly." The expression of gentleness and empathy on Sam's face as she addressed the little boy touched John's heart. "This is the kind of nice person I was talking about when I said police officers are your friends, Danny. He wasn't trying to hurt you. He was trying to help you."

Tears were sliding down the child's flushed cheeks. "Daddy hit him."

"Yes, he did. And he's going to be in trouble for doing that," Samantha explained. "It's not right to hit."

"My daddy hits me."

"We know," she said. "You don't have to talk about it anymore right now if you don't want to."

John was puzzled until she turned her glance his way and explained, "The court order came through via fax while I was in the office a few minutes ago. Danny won't be going home until the authorities determine it's totally safe for him there."

From the doorway there came a sharp intake of breath. Auburn-haired Lindy Southerland, Ben's wife, was standing there, trembling and gaping at them as if she couldn't decide whether to stand her ground or turn and flee.

Danny spied her, shouted, "Mama!" jumped off the bed, raced across the room and leaped into her open arms.

She held him close for a few moments, whispered soothing words and stroked his back to comfort him, then looked up.

There were tears in her wide, green eyes when she focused on Samantha and John to ask, "What do you mean he can't go home? What have you done to my baby?"

TEN

The timely arrival of social worker Brenda Connors saved Samantha from having to explain the details of the legal protection order to the distraught mother.

Instead, Sam stuck with John to make sure he was going to be all right. As soon as he had spoken with the first of the newly arrived officers regarding his role in the altercation, she took his arm and directed him down the hall to the E.R.

While Samantha was helping fill out the necessary paperwork, another nurse ordered him onto a gurney, took his vitals and put an ice pack on his temple.

Samantha was pleased to see that his color was good when she rejoined him a few minutes later. "How do you feel?"

"Besides embarrassed, you mean?" He winced and shifted the ice pack.

"Yeah. Besides that. Any headache, blurred vision, other unusual symptoms?"

"Not that I can tell." He started to try to get up.

"Hold it, mister. You can't go anywhere until a doctor sees you."

"You know as much as a guy like Weiss would. What became of him, anyway?"

"Last I heard he was cooling his heels in the staff lounge, sitting there talking to himself."

"Good. I'd rather not end up as his patient. He's probably so mad at me he'd slap me in the hospital just for spite."

She shook her head slowly, thoughtfully. "No, he wouldn't. He may be fooled by his buddy Ben, but he's still a good doctor. He won't order any tests or treatment he's not certain you need."

The curtains parted and a younger medical man entered. "Who won't? Are you two conspiring in here?"

Smiling a greeting and feeling immensely relieved, she introduced the two men in spite of their official name tags. "John, this is Dr. Adams. He's new to our staff."

To her surprise, her old friend began to eye the broad-shouldered, dark-haired physician as if he were sizing up a rival. *Well, well.* That was an interesting reaction. It would also be an encouraging one if she were at all eager to renew their formerly close relationship.

She wasn't, of course. John Waltham had made his position clear. In thinking back over their recent conversations, she tried to recall one of the many instances when he'd insisted that any attention he paid to her was purely business. For example…

Samantha almost choked. At that moment she could not bring one single incident to mind. Not one. There had to be some, of course. Otherwise, she'd have to admit that their lack of emotional connection since John's return to Serenity was entirely her doing.

That could not possibly be the correct conclusion. She had been the one who'd been left behind. She was the injured party in all this. Wasn't she?

Dr. Adams scribbled something on a clipboard, then told John he'd be discharged if no other symptoms appeared in the ensuing half hour.

Fifteen minutes later, Walt stuck his head between the curtains of the exam cubicle. Samantha took one look at the grin splitting his weathered face and guessed he'd come to gloat.

"Lose something, hotshot?" the older man drawled, clearly enjoying his chance to get in a dig.

"Temporarily misplaced my weapon," John replied with a wry grimace. "Has there been any sign of it?"

"Nope. Not so far. The chief is still trying to get a straight story out of the doc who witnessed the attack. According to him, you egged Southerland on and the guy just snapped."

Samantha's ire rose. "That is *so* not true!"

"We figured as much. What none of us can understand is how a bean counter got the drop on you."

"John was protecting a little boy," Samantha insisted. "If he hadn't turned aside when he did, that blow would have hit the child."

"You don't say."

"I most certainly *do* say. I saw the whole thing."

"Okay. Since you were a witness, too, we'll need your statement. I'll go tell the chief."

"Fine. You do that."

Samantha planned to keep some details of her involvement to herself rather than air them needlessly. When it came time to be specific, however, she was going to have to admit that she had only arrived in time to see Southerland hit John and had not been privy to whatever had occurred in the minutes prior to the blow.

"How are you really feeling?" Samantha asked him as a physician's assistant began to check him over one last time and signed off on his head trauma.

"Dumb. Foolish. Inept. Clumsy. Careless. And I'm sure Walt could add a few more choice opinions. Shall I go on?"

"I think that about covers it. I'm glad you haven't lost your sense of humor."

"I'd trade it for my gun right about now." He grimaced. "I can't believe the guy got away with it. I've had hardened criminals try moves like that and fail. Now it'll go on my record that an untrained civilian disarmed me. How will something like that look on my résumé?"

"Like you're human." Samantha sighed. Her own head was pounding and she'd missed supper, but there were more important things on her mind than personal comfort.

She laid a hand lightly on John's forearm to make sure she had his full attention. "I really do need to know how you feel. As soon as the chief is done with me I still want to visit Bobby Joe, if you think you're up to it."

Sliding off the edge of the exam table, John grasped both her hands. "Of course. We can kill two birds with one stone. I'll tell Levi you'll stop by tomorrow and see him, unless he wants to follow us to the station and take your statement tonight."

"Will I really be able to get into the jail? I

know I was out of line before when I insisted you had to break the rules for me. I really don't expect you to do that."

"We'll take a witness in with us. Somebody who's impartial. As long as you don't ask Bobby about his crime we should be okay. I figure the kid will have a court-appointed attorney once he's arraigned but I don't want to have to wait that long."

"Neither do I. We've lost a lot of time already."

Samantha felt him give her fingers a squeeze before releasing them. She knew she'd had her priorities straight when she'd put aside her search for Brutus to help Danny. It was just frustrating to be unable to do both tasks equally well.

The sun had set by the time they finished speaking with the chief and left the hospital. A waning crescent moon was masked by drifting clouds.

Samantha knew that Brutus's dark fur would be almost impossible to spot unless he happened to be standing under a streetlight—and there were none of those anywhere near her farm.

Each moment that brought her closer to the jail also increased her nervousness. Every muscle was taut, every nerve ending firing. Her head pounded. Her palms perspired. She wasn't afraid of the prisoner, himself; she was afraid he could not, or would not, help her.

They'd corralled Walt and asked him to meet them at the station. Samantha wasn't thrilled to have to include the older cop as a witness but since she'd known him all her life, she figured he'd be a better choice than Glenn or Chief Kelso, not to mention Sheriff Allgood, who had a well-earned reputation as a curmudgeon's curmudgeon.

They passed through the first locked door and into a dingy hallway lined with several small cells. The antiseptic-smelling place was nothing like the impressive pictures she'd seen of federal prisons, other than sharing a somber atmosphere that was so depressing it made her shudder.

The forlorn-looking youth sitting cross-legged on a gray blanket atop his cot might have brought a surge of sympathy under other circumstances. Not this time. She figured Bobby Joe's partners in crime were behind Brutus's disappearance and that assumption seriously dampened her usual compassion.

He looked up as Sam paused outside the cell. John and Walt flanked her. The prisoner's eyes were red rimmed and his whole body trembled as if a web of tangled puppet strings were jerking at it.

Recognition was slow in coming. He swung his legs off the cot and perched on its edge while he squinted at her. "Sa-Samantha?"

"Hello, Bobby Joe."

"Did my sisters send you?" There was a hopeful tone to the question.

"No. Nobody sent me. I came to ask if you knew who took my dog."

"Your what?"

She clamped her teeth on her lower lip to stop it from quivering before she continued. "You heard me. My dog. Somebody broke into my house. My old dog is missing."

His shoulders slumped and he leaned his elbows on his knees, his hands clasped between them. "I thought you came to spring me."

"You haven't had any other visitors?" she asked.

"Nope. I guess Mamaw is good and mad at me for lettin' little Jess get into my stuff." He cupped his face in his hands. "You've gotta believe me. I never intended for the kid to get sick."

"I don't want to talk about your problems," Samantha said after John prodded her with his elbow and shook his head in warning. "All I want to know is who might try to get back at you through me."

"Why should they do that?" Bobby Joe whined.

"Because one of your buddies apparently thinks you passed something to me and he wants it back." She held up her hand like a crossing guard stopping traffic when he opened his mouth to speak. "I don't care what he thinks you gave me or where it really is. All I need is a name. A clue. Something that will help me find Brutus."

"Who?"

"Her dog," John interjected.

"Oh."

"Well?" Samantha was running out of patience. "Look, Bobby Joe, you said you brought the little boy to me because you knew I'd help. I did. We saved his life. Don't you think you owe me something after that?"

His thin shoulders shrugged. "Yeah. I guess. Just don't tell nobody where you heard this or my life won't be worth a plug nickel."

"I'm already in trouble for keeping my mouth shut because of you, but you have my word."

"What about them?" the young man asked, pointing to John and Walter.

"We'll wait outside," John offered, taking the older deputy by the arm and urging him back down the hallway so they were out of sight without being out of hearing.

As soon as Samantha was ostensibly alone with the prisoner he arose and edged closer to the bars. "I'm about to jump out of my skin here. You got any pills on you? I figure a nurse…"

"No!" She took a step back, careful to stay beyond his reach. "Just level with me so I can go find my dog."

"Okay, okay. It was worth a try. I don't know nothin' about no dog. If I was lookin' for trouble I'd check that bar out in Moko. You know the one."

"There's no bar in Moko," Samantha argued. "Fulton County's dry. Nobody sells liquor here."

"Not in the town," the young man said, speaking as if he considered her dumber than dirt. "A little past it. Across the Missouri line."

"You think they'd take my dog all the way out there?"

"How should I know? You wanted to know where I'd go if I wanted to ask questions and I told you."

"All right. Thanks," she said, wondering if she'd gotten any information that was even close to the truth. At this rate she was grasping at straws but anything had to be better than just giving up.

After she rejoined her companions and they went back to the small, dimly lit office, Walt bid them good-night and clocked out. There was no one else on duty except Elaine, one of the mutual dispatchers for fire, police and the sheriff, and she was sequestered inside the locked radio room.

"Do you think the kid told you anything useful?" John asked Samantha.

"I strongly doubt it. What do you know about a bar, across the Missouri state line, a little past Moko?"

"Nothing. Why?"

"Bobby Joe said we should ask there about Brutus, but I think he was trying to send us on a wild-goose chase."

"That's out of my jurisdiction, anyway. How about visiting his family? They might know who he was hanging around with."

"True. I don't know why I didn't think of doing that sooner."

"Because you're too worried to think straight." John cupped her elbow as he escorted her to his truck. "I'm not at the top of my game, either." He patted his empty holster. "As you can see."

"Will you get your gun back when they find Ben Southerland?"

"I sure hope so. I've carried that same Glock ever since I got my badge."

Pausing, she looked him up and down. "Speaking of badges, why don't we swing by my place and change clothes before we do anything else? Even without a gun, you look *way* too official for visiting somebody who has a drug addict in their family."

John rolled his eyes theatrically, his grin wide. "You think?"

The change of clothing was simplified by the fact that John had already transferred some of his personal possessions to the travel trailer. Therefore, he was not only able to don suitably worn jeans and a T-shirt, he had a holster for his smaller holdout gun that slipped easily into his waistband at the small of his back where it didn't show.

"About time." Sam slammed the kitchen door, flew off the porch and joined him in the yard before he had time to fetch her. "Let's go."

"I take it you know where Bobby Joe lives," John said, starting his truck.

"Yes. Head through town, go past the square then take the 395 cutoff. Their home place is that big, old, brick house on the left about five miles out."

"That description rings a bell. Only I don't remember the name Boland being associated with it."

"It's a long story. Bobby Joe's two half sisters were taken in by their grandmother, Opal Fox, years ago, but they're grown now. She added the three teenage boys shortly after you left for Texas."

"Fox? Any relation to Charlie?"

"I think he may be Opal's grandnephew or a distant cousin. Why?"

"Because Charlie is a part-time sheriff's deputy."

"Well, don't hold his extended family against him," Sam warned. "If you did that to every person in this little town you'd soon suspect everybody of something."

"I suppose you're right. Charlie has always seemed to be on the up-and-up."

"Of course he is. I certainly wouldn't want my reputation to be based on my parents' actions. It's bad enough that my dad shows up in jail on a DUI once in a while. He used to phone me to bail him out but I refused often enough that he apparently got the message. He mostly stays home to get drunk these days."

Her matter-of-fact statement dredged up memories of their past; memories that were poignant even now. Chancing a sidelong glance at her, John noted the jut of her jaw, the stiffness of her spine and the way her hands were clenching the strap of the purse that lay in her lap.

Of course she had a wall built around her emotions. In her position, with her background, who wouldn't? The sad part was that he had once held the keys to that wall, had had her un-fettered, unguarded trust. He knew he had. And he had somehow lost that emotional connection.

Was it all his fault? He doubted it. There were some quirks to Samantha's personality that had always been hard to anticipate and equally hard to overcome. He knew their current problems were not simply a case of their original dis-agreement being carried over into the present. That may have been the case when they'd ini-tially met after the hostage crisis in the E.R., but that wasn't all there was to it now.

She glanced his way and caught him star-ing. He averted his gaze. This was not the right time for a heart-to-heart with her no matter how strongly he wanted to talk through their differ-ences. That would come later. He could wait. He'd force himself to bide his time, unlike the way he'd acted years ago when he'd kept press-ing her to marry and leave town.

It had floored him when she'd refused. Given her recent assertion that she'd believed he was making a mistake, he supposed he could under-stand her point of view. While he was trying to protect her, she was attempting to do the same thing for him.

What would it take to convince her she was still wrong about his motives? he wondered.

That question made him snort in self-disgust. The first thing he had to do, way before he tried to convince Sam that he was right, was convince *himself* of it. The way his head was spinning and his emotions kept taking unexpected roller-coaster rides, he wondered if he had the slightest idea what was truly best.

Would it be kinder to keep his distance? Could he do that? Was he even willing to give it a try?

John nodded to affirm the purity of his motives, yet there remained a niggling uncertainty in his mind that refused to go away. Considering the way he cared for Sam, even now, he wasn't sure his personal desires were not unduly influencing him.

"It's that house over there," Samantha said, pointing off the road. "Slow down and get ready to turn."

Her words jerked him back into the present and he steeled himself for the coming confrontation. "Okay. I'll park a ways from the house and walk up. You stay in the truck until I call you."

"You must be joking."

"Not at all. I'll explain what we need and then…"

Sam was already opening the door and preparing to get out as he stopped. The determined look she flashed his way left no room for negotiation.

"Come to think of it, I have a better idea," John said with a wry grin. "Why don't we work *together?*"

She chuckled. "Now you're making sense. For a change."

ELEVEN

Weeds in parts of the unkempt yard stood knee-high, some still green, some already drying out and dropping seeds in preparation for the coming winter. In other areas, where the grass had been repeatedly trampled, the dry, clay soil showed through.

Judging by what she could see offhand, Samantha concluded that the house was in desperate need of a coat of paint as well as repairs to its structure.

A couple of mottled-gray, cur dogs roused themselves from a spot beneath the sagging wooden porch and began to bark in chorus.

Samantha wasn't deterred. "The family knows me," she told John. "Let me go on ahead. I'll wave, if and when I need you."

"You sure?"

"Positive. Give me a chance. I can do this."

"Okay. Stay outside even if they invite you in. I'll be right behind you."

Although the Fox house appeared to be abandoned, Sam knew it wasn't. Everything had looked pretty much the way it currently did for as long as she could remember.

The dogs greeted her fearless approach as if she belonged there, tucked their stubby tails and lowered their heads in submission, acting embarrassed that they might have failed to recognize an old friend. Speaking quietly she paused only long enough to let them sniff her ankles before proceeding up onto the porch and rapping on the frame of the screen door.

The elderly, bent, arthritic woman who answered her knock gave her a quizzical look before breaking into a grin and pushing open the rickety screen. "Is that you, Samantha? Land sakes, girl. Where you been keepin' yourself?"

"I work at the hospital, Miss Opal. You remember, don't you?"

"Ah, that I do." Her smile faded as she pulled the sides of her sweater tighter and folded her arms to keep the garment in place as she stepped outside. "I heard you was there when Bobby Joe's foolishness made poor little Jess so sick."

"Yes. How's the baby doing?"

"Fine, praise the Lord. Went home with his mama over in Gepp after he got out of the hospital. Looks like everything'll be okay. All she has to do is go to court to prove she's a good mother and promise she won't make the mistake of leavin' him with somebody like Bobby Joe again."

Shaking her head slowly, sadly, Opal sighed and continued. "Beats me what happens to kids these days. Bobby was always a follower. I guess he picked the wrong friends. Thank goodness his sisters got married and moved away before it was too late for them, too. I did my best with all my grandkids but some were purely deaf to good Christian teachings."

Laying a hand of comfort on Opal's thin shoulder, Samantha asked, "What about his brothers? Are they still staying with you?"

"Only Marty. And Bobby Joe, of course. Jimmy enlisted a couple of months ago and he's gone off to boot camp. I dearly wish Bobby Joe had gone with him. I know it can be dangerous, bein' a soldier, but fryin' his brains with that dope he keeps usin' has got to be worse."

Although Samantha assumed Bobby Joe's history of drug abuse would keep him out of the military, she didn't argue.

Instead, she leaned to the side to peer into the house. "Is Marty home? I'd like to say hello to him, too."

"Nope. I reckon he's at work."

"Where does he work?"

"Here and there. Times are tough. I told him

to stay in school but he wouldn't hear of it. And now look at him. Can't hardly find a job, let alone keep one."

"When do you expect him home?"

The old woman shrugged. "Beats me. He's usually with Bobby Joe, but since…"

Samantha tensed and once again lightly patted Opal's shoulder through her snagged, fraying sweater. "I know you did the best you could with all your grandchildren. Anybody can see that. But right now I have a problem and I don't know who else to ask for help."

Looking into Opal's keenly focused blue eyes she caught a glimpse of the strong person who had accepted a responsibility that was not hers and had sacrificed her own comfort to make a home for her abandoned grandchildren.

The older woman reached for Samantha's hands and clasped them both. "Ask away. If there's anything I can do to help you I will."

"I'm afraid it all goes back to when little Jess was brought to the hospital. Somebody seems to think Bobby Joe gave me a package when he was there and they're doing all kinds of awful things to get me to give it back. Only I don't have it. I never saw anything like that."

"What can I do?"

"I don't really know," Samantha said. "I was hoping you or Marty might have some idea who was giving me such grief." Her voice broke and she cleared her throat before continuing. "They stole my dog, Miss Opal. I'd do just about anything to get him back but I can't hand over something I don't have."

"'Course you can't. You leave this to me. I'll find out what's goin' on or know the reason why. Mark my words, if Marty's involved he'll have me to deal with."

"Thank you," Samantha said. A solitary tear trickled down her cheek and she swiped it away before signaling John to join them.

"I'd like you to meet an old friend of mine, Miss Opal."

The wrinkles around her eyes tightened and she peered at him as he jogged up to join them. "Hah! I know you," she said. "Used to be a scrawny kid." With a grin she eyed him, head to toe. "Filled out pretty good, if I do say so myself. No wonder Sam's out and about again."

John offered his hand and Mrs. Fox took it. "Again?"

"Yep. Haven't seen hide nor hair of her in years and here she is, right on my doorstep. I figure somethin' musta changed."

"I told you. I just want to find my dog," Samantha insisted.

Opal cackled. "I heard you. See that you stick to that story and maybe other folks won't think anything of it but I ain't no fool. I've been around the block a few times. I know romance when I see it."

"You're wrong," Samantha said. John echoed her denial.

However, as soon as they bid the elderly woman goodbye and headed back to the truck, they heard her start to chuckle again.

"See what I meant before?" Sam said. "That's exactly the kind of thing we can expect if we're seen together too often."

"Are you trying to tell me to get lost?"

"No! I never meant anything like that. I was just saying…"

"That you don't relish being seen with me. I heard you loud and clear. And as soon as you get Brutus back and we figure out who's trying to hurt you, I promise I'll keep my distance."

That had not been her aim when she'd spoken, yet at this point she didn't know how to contradict his erroneous conclusion without admitting how she really felt. There had been times since John's return to Serenity when she had wished he'd stayed away, but those instances were getting more and more rare. Now, she found herself looking forward to seeing him again, to hearing his voice, to feeling the strength of his hand holding hers.

Sneaking a quick peek at him she noted the

firm set of his jaw, the stiffness of his posture, the way his strong hands gripped the steering wheel. His feelings were hurt, all right. And she had been the direct cause. Never mind all the times she had cried herself to sleep and blamed him for her unhappiness. That was then and this was now.

Samantha had almost mustered enough courage to try to explain her confused feelings when John asked, "Where to?"

"I don't have a clue. Should we try the bar Bobby Joe mentioned?"

"No. If anybody goes there it'll be me. And I'll be alone. Got that?"

"You don't have to raise your voice."

"I wasn't. I was merely stating a fact."

"Fine."

It had occurred to her more than once that she was too reliant on John for many things, including transportation. Whether or not she planned to obey his orders to the letter, she still needed wheels.

Waiting what she felt was a suitable period of time, she finally brought up the subject of the old car Elvina had left in the barn.

"Why don't we go back home and eat supper? Then, afterward, maybe you can have a look at Elvina's car for me the way you'd suggested. I can't afford to buy anything right now and I hate having to ask you to drive me to and from work all the time."

"Insurance should cover your loss," John said flatly.

Samantha made a face at him. "It would if I'd had that kind of coverage. After my car was paid off, all I kept was liability."

"Maybe the department will pay for your car since it was technically in our custody. I'll ask tomorrow."

"Thanks."

Pausing, she tried to decide if she was pushing too hard or if he was accepting her story. She truly did need a car. And he had been the first to mention it. Therefore, she felt she was on pretty solid footing.

"I have some chicken in the freezer. We could…"

John interrupted. "No, thanks. I'll grab a quick bite and get started going over Elvina's old car. That way I'll know if it needs parts and I can pick them up in town tomorrow."

"All right. I'll give you a blank check."

When his head snapped around and he stared across the seat at her she saw both anger and disappointment in his expression.

"I'll get the parts, Sam. It's the least I can do since we were responsible for the loss of your car."

"Nonsense. You didn't burn it," she argued.

"No, but it was destroyed on my watch. That has to mean something, even if you don't want to accept my help."

"I never said anything of the kind."

Judging by the way his jaw snapped shut he was still good and miffed. Well, too bad. She was doing her best to cope with multiple problems and his short temper was the least of her worries. She had an abused child to protect, a stolen dog to locate, one or more bad guys to outwit and goodness knows what else that she had yet to discover. Given all those things, John's snit fell very low on her list of priorities.

Still, when she looked at him and saw his distress it caused a genuine ache in her heart. She might refute her feelings all day long but they existed.

In truth, this was not a surprise. Denial was futile. Useless. She'd known the moment she'd laid eyes on him again. The love she'd thought was long gone, that had been banished forever, was very much alive.

Entering the house without being greeted by Brutus made Samantha's loss even more poignant. Yes, she had human friends, especially the wonderful support system at work, but Brutus had been the heart of her home, the creature who was always glad to see her, who never misunderstood her sometimes changeable moods.

She swiped away a stray tear. If she missed him this much already, what was it going to be like if she never got him back? That notion was devastating.

Rather than give in to sadness she quickly grabbed a granola bar, opened a can of soda for herself and picked up a second one to take to John.

As promised, he was in the barn. He'd removed the tarp that had covered the enormous, dark green sedan and had its hood up.

"What's the diagnosis. Will she live?"

"Probably. After a little CPR—Car Parts Resuscitation."

The joke wasn't all that funny but it gave Samantha reason to smile because it showed a lifting of her old friend's mood. "Good to hear. I brought you a soda."

He accepted it, popped the top and tipped it up for a long drink. "Thanks."

"You're welcome. I suppose I'd better grab some rags and start on the inside." She grinned more widely. "You have evicted all the mice, haven't you?"

"Most of them." His sardonic smile made her chuckle.

"Lovely," she said. "Now all I have to do is

adjust to being seen tooling around town in that barge. When Elvina drove it she could hardly see over the steering wheel. At least I'm tall enough that I won't have to sit on a pillow."

"You'll look just like a cute little old lady when you're behind the wheel," John countered. He stood back and wiped his hands on a rag before taking another swig of the canned drink she'd brought him. "We could paint flames on the sides. That would help your image."

"I'll pass. Hopefully I won't have to drive it for long."

"Actually, it's something of an antique. You might be able to sell it, if you have the title, and buy something else with that money."

"Now, there's an idea. I'll give it some thought." She gestured at the motor. "Does it run?"

"We'll soon find out. I replaced the old gas and put the battery from my truck in it until we can get you a new one. The oil looks clean but the tires are all flat. Chances are they'll have to be replaced unless they hold air better than I think they will."

"That's all minor stuff, right?"

"Yes." He pointed to the driver's seat. "Hop in and turn it over for me. Don't crank on it too long, though. I need my battery back in good shape."

"Right."

The door wasn't as hard to open as she'd expected it to be. Sliding behind the wheel brought back memories of her teen years when her benefactor had taught her to drive.

She made sure the car was in Park, then turned the key. The engine coughed, sputtered and came to life. Samantha saw surprise on John's face that equaled her own. "Wow. It sounds pretty good."

"Shut it off for now," he shouted, waving. "I want to have the oil changed and get a lube job before you drive it. We can have a garage pick it up tomorrow and see to the tires at the same time."

"I really am sorry to cause you all this trouble," Samantha said, getting out of the car and returning to his side. "But I'm also glad I have your help to figure out what's going on. We make a pretty good team."

"I used to think so," he said, sobering.

What could she say to that? No matter how badly she wanted to argue with him, his attitude would ensure that her words fell on deaf ears. As Elvina used to say, "It'd be like talkin' to a stump."

John handed her his empty soda can and backed away, clearly done with the car *and* with their conversation.

"Okay. I'll finish cleaning out the inside tonight so it's ready to go," she said. "See you in the morning."

At least he waved as he turned away and headed for his trailer, Samantha mused. She supposed she was fortunate to have received that much show of familiarity.

What she wanted—what she really wanted—was to step into his embrace the way she had when she'd been weeping for Brutus, but she knew better than to hope for the impossible. There were some dreams that were so outlandish that no amount of wishing or even praying would make them come true.

John slammed the tinny trailer door behind him. With the lights off he was able to watch the barn without being seen, just in case Samantha had another uninvited visitor. Chances were that no one would return. Not after all they'd already done. Even the dullest, most drug-addled mind should be able to reason that if Sam had had Bobby Joe's stash she would have turned it over to the police by now.

Nevertheless, he kept his vigil. Saw her go into the house then walk back to the barn carrying a bucket and an armload of rags. He wanted to be out there with her. To have her within reach, close enough to touch, to kiss…

Disgusted, he pulled his thoughts back into the realm of reality. No way was he going to kiss Sam, or even let himself think about doing so. It was bad enough that he had to be around her so much due to this assignment. Letting his imagination take flight was worse than foolish. It was self-destructive.

Slumping into a swivel chair and getting comfortable, he propped up his feet as he continued to monitor the activity in the barn. Sitting in semidarkness soothed his nerves and calmed his turbulent thoughts.

Sam was who she was and he was who he was. Trying to pretend he was someone else was foolish. So was expecting her to change to please him. Either they managed to accept each other without reservations or they didn't. It was as simple as that.

Weariness made John's eyelids heavy. Light from the barn threw an arc that illuminated the yard all the way to the house and overlapped the fainter glow from the small porch light that hung by the back door. It wasn't nearly as bright out as he'd have liked, even with the nearly full moon, but it would do.

Unable to walk around or change his position much without taking the chance of revealing his watchfulness, he fidgeted.

Sleep encroached, beckoned, tempted him.

He shook it off over and over, refusing to yield. "Come on, Sam. Go back into the house and lock the door, will you?" he muttered, rubbing his eyes with his knuckles.

Finally, he saw her starting to gather up her cleaning supplies. "About time, woman. That car must be as sterile as an operating room by now."

He leaned forward and scanned the empty yard. Nothing was moving except a flock of moths and other night-flying insects that had been drawn to the outside lights.

John yawned. Stretched. Looked away for a few seconds while he untied his boots and slipped them off.

The barn went dark. He peered out, expecting to see Samantha walking toward him. His brow furrowed. Where was she? She should be right there, right now.

Kicking aside the boots, he lunged for the door, threw it open and leaned out. "Sam?"

She didn't answer. He stepped down. The hair on his neck prickled a warning and he reached behind him to draw his holdout gun.

"Samantha!"

He froze, listening to the chirping of nocturnal insects and the calls of frogs in nearby ponds and gullies.

Nothing was moving. No one answered him.

Whip-poor-wills that had been singing before were now silent.

The still night air pressed in on him with smothering weight. Then he heard it. A scuffling sound. It only lasted for an instant but it had definitely come from the barn.

Ruing the fact that he was in his stocking feet he ignored the gravel-strewn driveway as he crossed it. Suddenly, something clanged like the echo of a pail connecting with another metal object. The car?

John flattened himself against the front wall of the old barn and cupped one hand around his mouth. "Samantha Rochard, if that's you in there you'd better speak up because I'm armed and I'm about to come in shooting."

He heard a gasp, a noisy whoosh of air and a deep voice expressing an opinion that was less than sterling.

The bucket connected again, only this time with a dull whomp followed by the clatter of it hitting the floor.

"Sam!"

"In here!" she screeched. "Hurry! He's getting away!"

Taking no thought for his own safety John pointed his weapon to the rafters, dashed through the doorway in a partial crouch and barreled straight toward the sound of her voice.

She flew into his arms, holding so tightly he could hardly draw a breath.

He shoved her behind him for protection and stood firm, aiming into the blackness. "Where did he go?"

"Out the back. I hit him over the head with the bucket when he tried to grab me and he took off."

Keeping one arm around her waist, John braced himself for an attack that didn't materialize. He could see that Samantha's eyes were wide, even in the dimness of the barn.

"Aren't you going to go after him? Shoot him or something?" she asked.

So relieved he could hardly catch his breath, John shook his head. "Not this time, lady. All I plan to do is get you into the house where you'll be safe and then notify the station. Again."

"Isn't that why Levi and Harlan put you out here in the first place? Aren't you the officer on duty?"

Chagrined, John sighed. "Yeah. I am. And the next time you need me I hope I'm closer at hand than I was tonight."

"You must have been watching me or you wouldn't have known I was in trouble."

"Apparently I wasn't watching closely enough," John told her while he escorted her to her door.

"From now on, where you go, I go, at least when we're home."

"Home?"

"Yes. Home." He turned to face her. "I seem to have problems concentrating properly when I'm thinking about you. I figure the best way to deal with that is to become your shadow."

Seeing her jaw drop for a few seconds before she snapped it closed, he realized that up until now she'd had no idea how much her constant presence had been unhinging him.

"Really?" It was a breathless question, more whisper than word.

"Really," John said.

He held his ground when she leaned closer. Her face was raised, her eyes misty.

If she had been merely a needy crime victim he could have easily stepped away from her. But this was Samantha. His Samantha. And she was looking at him as if…

Sighing, he closed his eyes, surrendered to the urges he'd been fighting for so long, leaned down and kissed her.

TWELVE

Moments later, left standing alone in the middle of her kitchen, Samantha stared at the back door as it closed after John.

She was stunned. Although she knew what had just happened, she couldn't rationalize it. He had kissed her, that much was certain. The question was, *Why?*

And why had he looked startled and immediately pushed her away? Had he been as flabbergasted by their emotional connection as she was? That was certainly possible, given their history and the way they were clearly still attracted to each other. For a few, beautiful seconds she had felt as if no time had passed. As if nothing had changed between them.

No, she corrected, shivering. Something *had* changed and whether or not it was for the better was beyond her reasoning. If anything, their emotional connection was deeper, more poignant.

This time, John's kiss had moved her in a way

that it never had before, even when he had bid her that final goodbye before leaving Serenity so long ago. It was as if their love had grown in the ensuing years instead of faltering and fading the way she had assumed it would. That, alone, was enough to take her breath away and make her heart race. Considering the possibility that he might share the same impression was mind-boggling.

Samantha meandered to the sink and leaned her palms on the edge of the countertop while staring out the window at the travel trailer. John's abrupt departure after their solitary kiss only made sense if he was either sorry or glad.

"Now that's a logical conclusion if I ever heard one," she muttered, chuckling to herself at the absurdity of her thoughts.

Another good question was how *she* felt. That was even harder to discern. Yes, she had relished his kiss. And, no, she had not sought it. Or had she? If memory served, she hadn't done much to deter him. As a matter of fact…

Disgusted with herself, she turned away from the window and headed for the refrigerator. Medically speaking, hypoglycemia from lack of food had probably muddled her thinking processes. What she needed was a decent meal, not a renewed relationship with someone who had already proved he was unreliable by abandoning her for the sake of his career.

Samantha pulled open the door to the fridge and leaned down to peer in. Only one thing caught her attention. A note lay on the closest shelf. One corner of it was weighted down by a carton of milk.

With a trembling hand she started to reach for the paper, then stopped herself, pulling back as if her hand had been burned. The message was crystal clear from right where she stood and if there were any clues on the note, such as fingerprints, she didn't want to smudge them.

"The package for the dog." That was all it said. It was enough.

Without stopping to consider her own safety, Samantha straight-armed the back door and sailed down the steps.

She circled the trailer and pounded on it, rattling the metal door in its frame. "John!"

The small revolver was in hand again when he confronted her. "What is it? What happened this time? Is the prowler back?"

"No." She waved her hands wildly. "I found another note! In the house."

"Okay." Stepping down, he scanned the visible sections of the yard before he said, "Looks all clear this time. Show me what you found."

"They *did* take Brutus," she explained, lamenting the quaver in her voice as she led the way. "We were right. Somebody stole him. They said so."

Brightness from the kitchen spilled out onto the porch. John shoved Samantha into the house ahead of him and slammed the door. "Where is it? Show me."

"Over there. In the refrigerator. Right in front. I didn't touch a thing except the handle."

He followed her directions, then turned back to stare at her with a frown. "*Where* did you say you saw it?"

"Right in there. You can't miss it." Edging past him she pointed toward the shelf in question without actually looking at it. "They weighted it down with the milk carton. See?"

"No. I don't."

"What?" Sam peered around him, incredulous. "It was lying right there. I didn't imagine it. I saw it with my own eyes."

Reaching for his cell phone, he pointed his pistol into the kitchen, kept his back to Sam and made a call. "This is Waltham. I'm on scene at the Rochard residence. We've had another break-in."

He paused, listening. "No. This is in addition to the incident in the barn that I already reported. That's right."

Unable to hear the response from the dispatcher, Samantha was nevertheless able to tell they were taking the call seriously when John added, "Yes. I'm armed. I'll keep the victim safe until backup arrives."

Samantha leaned against the counter for support, wondering if her knees were going to continue to support her. What if she'd been alone when she'd found the note? What would she have done?

"You okay?" John's deep voice rumbled, sending a jolt of electricity along her nerves and making the hair at the nape of her neck prickle.

"No. I'm not okay," she answered bluntly. "Right this minute, I don't know if I'll ever be okay again."

When he said, "Good. That means you'll be more careful from now on," she didn't know what she wanted most: to slug him for giving her an unnecessary lecture or kiss him again for standing by her.

Considering the ambiguity of her feelings she decided that doing neither would be the smartest choice.

At least for the time being.

"I can't be positive," John told Charlie Fox, the young, part-time sheriff's deputy who had responded this time because he'd been patrolling nearby, "but it looks as if the dognappers decided to retrieve the ransom note as soon as they knew Samantha had seen it."

"Why bother?"

"I don't know. Nothing they've done so far has made a lot of sense. When we first missed Brutus we didn't spot any note but I'm not positive either of us thought to look in the refrigerator." He scowled. "That's my fault."

"Maybe. Or maybe they left it after that, when you were busy over at the hospital."

"Yeah, maybe." Coloring from remembered embarrassment, John shook his head. "Has there been any sign of Ben Southerland—or my Glock?"

"Not yet. We've expanded the APB to include all Arkansas counties and up into southern Missouri."

"Good."

"I can make a sweep through the house before I leave if you want." Fox looked pointedly at John. "Since you're camped here I don't suppose there's too much to worry about."

"That was supposed to be the general idea. I'll take care of the house."

"Nice gig if you can get it." The deputy touched the brim of his cap, then said, "G'night, folks. I'll let myself out and start on the yard while you're checking inside."

Their cursory walk-through didn't take long.

As soon as they heard the patrol car driving away Samantha looked to John. "You can go, too. I'm fine. Really."

"You weren't fine when you were beating on my trailer so hard the whole thing was shaking."

"Okay, so maybe I was a little excited."

"A little." He eyed the door. "Is it just me or are deputies getting younger and younger? Charlie didn't look old enough to shave."

"I think he's in his early twenties. You'd mentioned his name when we were going to see Opal. Hadn't you met him before?"

"No. He must have been off duty when I was given the station tour. It's not as if Chief Kelso or the sheriff threw a welcome-home party for me, although there was enough of a fuss that it ruffled a few feathers." John gestured toward the kitchen table. "Why don't you have a seat and tell me everything you can remember about that note?"

"Like what? You heard what I told Charlie."

"Humph. He's such a raw rookie I'm surprised he pinned his badge on right side up. There were some very important questions he didn't ask. For instance, was this note at all like the first one? Same paper, same lettering? Anything?"

"Well, it wasn't misspelled, although that may

have been done to the one before to try to throw us off."

"What was the exact wording?"

She squeezed her eyes shut for a moment, then repeated what she'd said earlier. "'The package for the dog.'"

"That's all? No instructions? No way to make contact?"

"No." Samantha's gaze searched his and she began to frown. "That doesn't make much sense, does it? If they want this mysterious package they're so sure I have, why not tell me how to get it to them?"

"Maybe there's another note hidden somewhere around here."

"Like where? Wouldn't we have found it already?"

"I don't know. There was no good reason for them to leave the threat in the fridge so we can't assume there will be logic to wherever they may have put further instructions."

The misty look in Samantha's eyes told him she was close to losing control of her emotions. That was perfectly natural, he simply didn't want to see her give in to grief before there was adequate reason to do so.

"Okay," John said, deciding they both needed to continue to be proactive, "here's what we'll do. We'll start in this room, since it's the site of the last contact, and go through everything. I want you to open the cupboards and look behind every pot and pan, every dish. Don't skip a thing."

"What if there's nothing here?"

"Then we'll move on to another room and then another, until we either run out of places to look or find something helpful."

Her voice was subdued and held a touch of melancholy when she simply said, "Thank you."

He had been about to reassure her by reminding her he was doing his duty when she looked straight at him to add, "And I promise you, John Waltham, if you dare tell me one more time that it's just your job, I will *scream*."

It wasn't only the defiant look in her eyes and the hands fisted on her hips that impressed him. It was also the challenge in her statement. Evidently, Sam was no longer buying his excuse that he was merely carrying out orders.

Truth to tell, sticking by her meant a lot more than that to him, too. A whole lot more.

Samantha was so frustrated, so weary, she almost asked John to take a break with her when they'd finished searching every nook and cranny in the kitchen.

Sighing, she straightened, empty-handed, and shook her head sadly. "There's nothing here.

We've been over the whole room and…" Her gaze drifted past his shoulder and settled on a hook by the door where she kept Brutus's leash. It was still hanging there, just as she'd left it. Her eyes widened as she began to truly observe. "The dog's collar! Look."

John whirled. "Was he wearing it when you last saw him?"

"Yes. I always keep it on him unless I'm giving him a bath." Pushing past her companion she grabbed the braided nylon and jerked it down. There was a piece of white paper, folded and taped to the rabies vaccination tag.

Her hands were shaking so badly she passed the collar to John. "Here. You look. I can't."

"Not without putting on gloves first. Stay right here. Don't move. I'll be right back."

Samantha doubted she could have taken a step if she'd wanted to. Her feet felt glued to the floor and her knees were once again threatening to give way and drop her in a useless heap.

The moment John returned from the trailer he slipped his hands into the thin gloves.

She thrust the collar at him. "Hurry."

"I am."

Watching him, knowing him so well, she could tell he was nearly as nervous as she was. Being a professional he was handling the anxiety better, of course, but it still showed. The look on his face when he unfolded the piece of paper held a mixture of anger and sorrow.

She grasped his wrist above the glove. "What is it? What did they say?"

"That you have until this coming Sunday night to comply with their demands."

"Or?"

His arm encircled her, supported her, and he pulled her to his side before he said, "Or they'll kill Brutus."

Unshed tears wet her lashes. "That's not fair. I can't even fake it if I don't know what this package is supposed to look like."

John laid the collar aside and closed her in his embrace.

At this moment in time she was beyond refusing to accept the support and consolation he offered. Brutus was going to die. And it was her fault.

She heard the rapid beats of John's heart. Her own echoed them as if they had somehow been synchronized. Latex snapped as he shed his gloves before stroking her hair and whispering comforting words.

"Hush. There has to be a way."

"What? What?"

"I don't know. When Bobby Joe was arrested he had nothing in his pockets except a dollar bill and some loose change. How could he have disposed of drugs unless he gave them to someone? The little boy was clean, too."

Samantha's head was whirling. She'd replayed the scene in the E.R. over and over in her mind, hoping to somehow see more than she had before.

She leaned away to look up at him. "There are only three possibilities. The hospital staff, your police buddies or the air ambulance that took Jess to Children's."

"The ambulance crew is out," John said. "Bobby Joe never got near it. Unless…" He planted a firm kiss in the middle of her forehead and grinned. "You're a genius."

"Why? What did I do?"

"Remember the stuff you were packing up to send with the little boy when I was talking to you at the hospital that first day? Did you go through it carefully or were you in too big a hurry to bother?"

"I just folded and bagged it the way I always do." She was starting to see what he was getting at. "Do you think Bobby Joe put something in with Jess's clothes?"

"More likely in the *quilt,*" John said with conviction. "I'll make a few calls and see what we can come up with. Keep your fingers crossed."

Samantha was grinning through her tears. "You're right. That has to be it. I remember thinking how cute that quilt was with little denim pockets and flaps and buttons sewn right into the design for toddlers to play with!"

Hopes soaring, she closed her eyes and thanked God while John phoned his station and explained his theory. They were right. They had to be. The police had gone over the E.R. with a fine-tooth comb and had discovered nothing. The same applied to the parking lot and the old car Bobby Joe had been driving. Therefore, whatever he'd been carrying on his person had to have been removed. And the only objects that had left the room other than the people, were the personal items in the plastic bag.

Hopefully, the mystery would be solved soon and she could welcome Brutus home with open arms.

John didn't know how to break it to her. The expectant look on Sam's pretty face was going to vanish the moment he spoke and he knew it. Nevertheless, he owed it to her to deliver the truth.

He cleared his throat. Took her hand. Held it tightly and willed her to receive the information calmly, if not happily. "We're too late. Whatever was at the hospital left when Jess did."

"Of course it did." Her lips pressed into a thin line. "Miss Opal said his mother had already taken him home. Naturally she'd have picked up his clothing and other belongings, too."

"Right. Which means we have no way to check other than to visit the woman and hope she'll cooperate."

"If she was as mad at Bobby Joe as I think she was, we may still have a chance."

John decided not to mention the possibility that the young mother was as involved in drugs as Bobby Joe had been. If that were the case and she'd found the stash amid her own son's clothing, she'd most certainly lie about it.

"How do you want to proceed?" John asked.

"I don't know. Do you think it would be best to let Opal handle this? She volunteered to help us."

"And she knows Jess's mother personally," John added. "Why don't you give her a call?"

Sam checked the time. "Because I think it's way too late at night. I don't want to upset her by waking her up."

"Now you're starting to sound just like you did when we were kids," John told her. "You spent your childhood being afraid of triggering your father's bad temper. I remember lots of times when you backed off in spite of being in the right." He paused for effect. "Don't do that this time, Sam. You'll never forgive yourself if you do."

The astonishment in her expression was followed quickly by clear resolve. "You're right. I had slipped back into my old habits." She reached for a phone book and thumbed it open. "I'll call Opal."

"Good. And I'll go get an evidence bag for this new note. If we end up going out we'll drop it off at the station."

"Do you think they'll take it seriously?"

"Yes," John said flatly. "This isn't just about a lost dog anymore. It's about drug trafficking. If we can catch whoever is so intent on getting Bobby Joe's stash and put them away, too, it'll be a win-win for the department."

"And save Brutus," Samantha said, holding her phone to her ear. She raised a hand just as John was about to answer. "Hello, Miss Opal," she began, "sorry to bother you so late. This is Samantha Rochard. Remember when you said you'd do anything to help me? Well, I have a favor to ask."

Listening to the story Opal told, Samantha began to tremble. Marty hadn't come home at all and his grandmother had no idea where he'd gone. Moreover, when the older woman had gone to check on Jess and his mother she'd found their house empty and looking as if its occupants had packed up and left in a hurry.

Sam's eyes met John's. She shook her head. "It's no use. Opal says she thinks Jess and his mother have split. Marty's missing, too. Our chances of finding the quilt, if that happens to be where the drugs are stashed, are nonexistent."

"Nothing's impossible for God," he countered.

Samantha made a face at him. "Now *you* sound like you did when we were teenagers. I told you then and I'll tell you again. If God had cared that much about me, He'd never have stuck me in that dysfunctional family in the first place."

"But He rescued you by sending Elvina into your life," John argued. "And when you were older, there was me."

"You?"

"Yes, me. I would have gladly taken you away with me. I don't know why you have so much trouble believing that, Sam. It isn't that the Lord failed to rescue you, it's that you refused His help when He sent it."

"I moved in with Elvina. It turned out that she needed me as much as I needed her."

"Then perhaps that's the way things were meant to be." Picking up the plastic bag containing the newest note, John said, "Sleep well. I'll be keeping watch."

"You have to sleep, too."

"I will. Charlie is going to stop by after he goes off duty tonight and take over for a couple of hours so I can get some shut-eye. I'll be fine. Night, Sam."

"I wish…"

She broke off before her heart could make her say something she'd be sorry for. This was the second time John had reminded her of his offer of marriage and she was beginning to see that their parting was as much her fault as it had been his.

That conclusion didn't sit well on her conscience. Not well at all. If she were to accept his version of their failed romance she'd have to admit too much culpability.

She'd also have to admit that maybe God hadn't forgotten her plight and left her so bereft that she'd wept for literally weeks. If John was right, their heavenly Father had had her best interests at heart all along.

More truths kept surfacing as if linked together by an unbreakable chain. As soon as she accepted one, another appeared, then another and another.

God had given her Elvina Prescott's love and care just when she'd needed it most.

God had offered her happiness as John's wife

and the main reason she'd failed to see that gift was because she'd been too self-centered.

And, if she were totally honest with herself, the reason she'd stopped attending church had far less to do with embarrassment than it did with her disappointment that the Lord had not seen fit to fix her life exactly the way she'd envisioned.

Astounded and more than a little disconcerted, she closed her eyes, bowed her head and prayed for forgiveness right where she stood.

THIRTEEN

The following two days passed with little change other than that their window of opportunity for rescuing Brutus was closing.

Sam went about her tasks at work and tried not to think about her poor dog all the time, yet there was rarely a moment that passed when her faithful canine companion wasn't in her thoughts—and yes, in her prayers.

There had been a slight delay in finding a suitable foster home for Danny Southerland so he had remained in the hospital temporarily. No one had seen hide nor hair of his father, Ben, since the man had fled. To everyone's dismay, the police had no leads.

Brenda Connors visited Danny daily, as did his mother, Lindy. It was evident that she didn't approve of the legal action that had usurped her parental rights but when Samantha had calmly explained how the system worked and had assured Lindy that she would be given her day in court, the timid woman had seemed to settle down and accept the inevitable.

In many ways, Samantha could identify with her. As Ben's wife and Danny's mother, Lindy had spent years tiptoeing through life and trying to keep the peace when she should have been enjoying motherhood.

Ever since Danny had been hospitalized, Sam had made it a point to stop by his room whenever she had a free moment. He wasn't her patient, per se, but the facility was small enough that she could easily visit. The more she did that, the more the child seemed to open up to her and the greater were her chances of being able to truly help him through her CASA work.

Sam viewed Lindy as a second victim. The trouble was, unless the young woman learned to stand up for her rights and those of her son, there was a chance a judge might permanently remove Danny from her home. And, until Ben was caught, that threat remained, as well.

Yawning, Samantha finished her paperwork for the day and clocked out. She was getting used to driving Elvina's old green barge of a car, undoubtedly because it reminded her of her late friend and mentor.

Calling good-night to the swing-shift nurses, she started for the rear door, then decided to stop by Danny's room, tell him she'd bring him a treat in the morning and ask what he'd like.

The door to one-ten was ajar and she could hear cartoons playing on the television.

Smiling, she entered—and froze. The child's bed was empty.

John was running late. He glanced at his watch. If one more person pulled out in front of him and kept him from getting to the hospital in time to escort Sam home he was going to be tempted to roll down his window and yell at them.

"Come on. Move it," he muttered, maneuvering his pickup in and out of traffic in a manner that would have earned a civilian a ticket from him if he'd been on traffic duty.

Wondering if Sam might like to share another pizza, he flipped open his cell and hit her number on speed dial. The ringing went directly to voice mail.

John scowled. "Hey, Sam," he grumbled into the empty cab. "Whoever you're talking to, hang up. We have plans to make."

He snorted in self-derision. "Plans? Hah! In your dreams, Waltham. In your dreams."

She was in his dreams, of course. And in nearly every waking thought. If he'd envisioned this strong a reaction to her he might not have come home. Then again, if it just so happened that Sam was starting to have tender feelings for him, too, maybe he'd made the right choice.

A large, dark vehicle swerved and passed him going in the same direction. Considering the speed at which John was traveling, the other guy had to be going sixty—in a thirty-five-mile-an-hour zone.

He peered after the disappearing SUV, hoping to get the license number, but it was impossible to see clearly enough. Instead, he grabbed his two-way radio and contacted the station.

"Dispatch, this is John Waltham."

"Copy. What's the problem?"

"I'm northbound on Highway 62 in my private vehicle, crossing Main. Some dude just blew by me like I was standing still. Do we have reports of robberies or assaults? Anything he could be running from?"

"Not recently," the dispatcher said pleasantly. "You don't have to work 24/7, you know. It is okay to kick back when you're off the clock."

"Yeah, I know. Just curious. Thanks."

The sleek, black vehicle was disappearing into the distance. It was through town now and therefore back into a fifty-five-mile-an-hour zone so it would probably not cause any accidents.

If he happened to catch up to that driver before he passed the hospital, however, he might stop the guy long enough to ask him where he was going in such an all-fired hurry.

Samantha checked the tiny bathroom in one-ten just to be sure she wasn't overreacting, then raced down the hallway to the nurses' station.

"Was the Southerland boy discharged?"

Her friend Alice scowled at her. "Not according to the early shift. You should know. There was a standing order to notify you if he was leaving."

"Well, his bed is empty and I can't find him," Samantha said, breathless. "Call the police. I'm going outside to see if I can track him down while you search in here. He might have gotten it into his head to try to go home on his own." Except in Danny's case she figured that home would probably be the last place he'd want to go, primarily because his father might be there.

What about Lindy? When had she last seen Danny's mother? Encountering her around the hospital had become so commonplace she wasn't positive. After lunch? Maybe. Maybe not. One thing was certain. She had not bid the woman goodbye or seen her leave the hospital, with or without her son.

"If I were Lindy, what would I do?" Sam muttered to herself. *Flee? Stand my ground?*

It didn't matter at this point. Wherever Danny was she hoped and prayed he was at least safe. If his mother had made off with him that was certainly better than having his father show up again.

It took Samantha little time to check the parking lot. Since it was between the afternoon and evening visiting hours there weren't many cars there.

"Think. Think," she told herself as she pivoted, studying the area to no avail. "What kind of car did she drive?"

The only vehicle Sam could recall was the silver luxury sedan the Southerlands had been using when she'd seen them in Ash Flat. Chances were good that that was Ben's car and his wife drove something far less ostentatious.

Fisting her keys, Samantha made her way to Elvina's old car and checked to be sure the backseat was empty before unlocking the doors and getting in. Her hands gripped the wheel. Where should she go? Where should she look first?

She decided to start by making easy circles around the hospital lot, then progress to driving up and down nearby streets before heading toward the Southerland residence. Lindy might be introverted but she was smart. She was a mother tiger protecting her cub. The likelihood that she'd take Danny to a home where both the authorities and his fugitive father might find him was slim.

"So, where did you go?" Samantha whispered to herself. "What would I do in your place?"

No earth-shattering answers came to her. She had been so overwrought when she'd discovered Danny was missing, she hadn't even thought to pray.

Now, cruising slowly down the narrow, tree-shaded streets, she remedied that oversight. "Father, help. I know I've fought You many times when I should have listened, but I'm not asking this for me, I'm asking it for Danny. Show me where to go. What to do. For the sake of a helpless little boy. Please."

Shadows danced in the shade along the country road as clouds scudded across the sky and the wind ruffled the leaves above.

A slightly built woman clad in black jeans, a designer T-shirt and matching cropped jacket held the hand of a thin child and hurried him along.

Samantha braked, studying the pair as she cruised slowly past. The woman's head was covered by a dark-colored scarf so she couldn't tell what color hair it masked, but the size and build of the child certainly fit Danny. The question was, why were they afoot? If Lindy was planning to escape, why not drive?

A nearby alleyway provided a convenient place to turn around. Samantha reversed directions and headed back to get a better look.

That was when she saw the men. There were two of them, one larger than the other. Both were clad in the nondescript clothing typical of that area: tattered jeans, faded shirts and lace-up hunting boots. Each was bulky enough to pose a serious threat even if unarmed, and they were approaching the woman and child warily, not as if they were merely passing in the street but as though they were preparing to accost her.

There was no doubt in Samantha's mind. She was about to witness an assault. It didn't matter who the victims were. She was duty bound to try to help them.

John was still trailing the speeding car that had caught his attention when he'd passed through town. He noticed it starting to slow.

He scowled when he thought he recognized Sam's car in the distance, as well. There was probably more than one ancient sedan like that running around Serenity, but given her penchant for getting herself into trouble, he figured there was a good chance she was involved in whatever was going on up ahead.

The highly polished black SUV braked so rapidly that John had to swerve to keep from rear-ending it. His trajectory carried him past. That's when he saw Sam. His jaw dropped.

She was standing beside another woman and bravely facing several very large men. If he hadn't seen it for himself he wouldn't have believed it.

Samantha whispered to Lindy behind her hand. "What were you thinking? Danny was safe in the hospital."

"He'll never be safe unless I take him away from here and hide him," the boy's mother replied.

"Who are these guys? What do they want?"

"I don't know. I left my car parked right here and when I came back for it, it was gone."

One of the men laughed sardonically. "Yeah. It was real nice of ya to bring the kid out to us like this. I thought we were gonna have to sneak into the hospital to spring him."

Samantha closed ranks with Lindy, pushing Danny behind them. "Leave us alone."

That made both of the attackers chortle. The apparent leader said, "Listen, lady, we don't want nothin' to do with you or your friend. All we want is Ben's kid."

"Did my husband send you?" Lindy asked.

"Not hardly. We want to find him as bad as the cops do. Now hand over the boy. We need him for bait." He spread his arms as if expecting the frightened women to simply cave in to the threat and deliver the child.

Samantha had other ideas. She took her eyes off the main assailant only long enough to whisper to Lindy, "When I make my move, you run for it."

There was agreement in the woman's teary glance. She swallowed hard and nodded.

Raising her own hands in mock surrender, Samantha took one step forward, then another, hoping she could work her way close enough to the man to be within kicking range. A person didn't have to have a medical background to know what method of assault would have the strongest effect.

"The kid," he demanded. "Quit stalling."

"Okay, okay," Sam drawled, hoping her voice wouldn't crack from fear. "Let's get this straight. You don't really want Danny, you want his father. So why not concentrate on Ben and leave us alone?"

"It's not that simple. Tell Southerland we just want to know where he put the money. He'll know what we mean. When we get those account numbers he can have his kid back."

Samantha shrugged and feinted as if she were

going to capitulate. She shifted her weight, then drew back one foot and let fly. The surprise kick caught the man below the waist and doubled him over.

Behind her, Lindy screamed. "Danny!"

"Mama!"

Sam whirled, ready to do battle. The moment she realized what was happening she started to run.

It was too little, too late. The second burly man had hold of Danny and was loading him into an SUV that had just pulled up. The guy Samantha had kicked shoved her out of the way, slid in with the child and slammed the door as the vehicle began to accelerate.

Lindy had been thrown to the ground. Samantha knelt beside her and touched her shoulder.

"Are you okay?"

The distraught mother lifted a face of anguish and stared, mute.

"Who *were* those guys?" Samantha demanded. "Think. You must know something that will help."

"I—I don't know their names," Lindy wailed. "I think I've seen Ben talking to them before but he never said who they were or what his connection was."

"Well, there has to be one."

Sam couldn't help but notice John running toward them. Judging by his expression he was more than worried. He was irate.

Rising, she held up her hand like a traffic cop. "Before you start yelling at me, you need to report a kidnapping. Those guys in the SUV just took Danny Southerland. They said he was their hostage."

"Why? What did they want?"

"Ben," Samantha said. "I don't know what he's mixed up in but it must be bad. They said they intended to use Danny for bait until Ben told them where he'd hidden some money he took from them."

"How did Danny get outside?" John demanded, reaching for the radio that was clipped to his belt. "And how in the world did *you* get involved?"

"It's a long story." Samantha took Lindy's arm and helped her to her feet. "They were apparently on their way to kidnap Danny when his mother decided to run away with him. Turns out she had the right idea, her timing was just a little off."

"We should have posted a guard on his room," John said, chagrined. "We would have if we'd suspected anything like this. I figured his only threat was from his father."

"What are we going to do?" Samantha asked,

keeping an arm around Lindy's shoulders while the woman sobbed uncontrollably, her face in her hands.

"Hang on." John spoke into his radio and cited all the details he had amassed before turning back to the women. "Sheriff Allgood and Chief Kelso are on their way. They're making arrangements to have the situation broadcast on local radio and TV stations in the hopes that Ben will respond."

"What if he doesn't?" Samantha asked.

"I got their license number when they stopped, thanks to the same SUV almost running me off the road on its way here. That's a good start, especially if the tags weren't stolen. We're setting up roadblocks on the highways."

"What can we do?" She was eyeing Lindy as she spoke. "There must be some way we can help."

"There is. You can come with me to the station and look at pictures of known criminals."

"Mug shots? Like in the movies?"

John shook his head at her naïveté. "These days we do all that by computer but the result is the same. First, I think you should take Mrs. Southerland to the E.R. and have her checked out." He grimaced. "It wouldn't hurt if you had yourself looked at, too."

"There is not a thing wrong with me," Samantha insisted.

She saw him shaking his head as he turned to walk back to his truck. He didn't have to verbally refute her to get his opinion across. He was unhappy with her actions, as usual. Well, that couldn't be helped. She had done the right thing and if she could go back in time and do it all again she wouldn't change a thing—except maybe to kick harder.

Of all the things she was, daughter, nurse and friend, her work as a CASA volunteer was the most important. And the toughest. There had been many times since she'd first enrolled in the program when she'd wondered if her heart was going to break for the children she was assigned to help.

Only the sense that she was carrying out a divine mission had kept her from giving up. The same sense would carry her through this catastrophe, too. It had to, because she knew that in her own strength she was as helpless as the waifs she was sworn to defend.

FOURTEEN

The next hour was spent in full crisis mode. John fielded questions from his chief and the sheriff while Samantha and Lindy sat together in the back of a patrol car and commiserated.

He'd been so upset, so frustrated, he'd avoided contact with either of them until he had calmed down. Whatever they'd gotten mixed up in was a lot more complicated than anyone had imagined. And whoever was out to get Ben Southerland now had the upper hand. Big-time.

Pausing beside the cruiser he rapped on the closed rear window and motioned for Samantha to come out and join him.

There was so much sadness and suffering reflected in her gaze when it met his he was instantly contrite. Slipping an arm around her shoulders, he guided her a short distance from the car, then checked to be sure Lindy had not followed before he began to speak.

"It doesn't look good," he confided. "There's been no sign of the kidnappers or the boy."

"What about Ben? He's the key to all this."

"We agree. If we could question him we might have more success. Until he either surfaces or acts on his own to rescue Danny, we're stymied."

"Do you think he will? I mean, he was the one who abused the boy, so why would he stick out his neck to save him?"

"I don't know that he would. But he is Danny's father. That has to count for something, even if he's a rotten excuse for a dad."

"Hmm. Maybe. Makes me wonder if my dad would have come to my rescue in a similar situation. I doubt it. He was usually too drunk to do much except raise a ruckus and then pass out."

"Do you see him often?"

"Almost never. He used to get stopped pretty regularly when he was making beer runs between home and the Missouri line. Then I'd get called to come and bail him out, particularly after Mom left. That hasn't happened lately."

"Maybe he's reformed."

She laughed cynically. "That'll be the day."

"What do you want to do next?" John asked, purposely changing the subject and gesturing toward the patrol car where Lindy waited. "Shall I have you taken home when you and Mrs. Southerland are through looking at mug shots?"

"I can drive myself." Raising her face and looking into his eyes as if trying to read his thoughts, Sam asked, "What about the druggies who took Brutus? Have you had any leads?"

"No. Sorry. I wish I had better news."

"And Danny comes first. That's how it has to be. I understand. A missing person case takes precedence."

To his chagrin, a tear escaped and slid down her cheek. She turned to whisk it away. "It's okay. Really it is. I just…"

John pulled her closer for a supportive hug. "I know. You miss him. So do I."

"Do you think he's still alive?"

"If my prayers are being answered the way I hope they are, yes."

"Thank you," Samantha whispered as she slipped her arms around his waist and laid her cheek on his chest. "I don't know how I'd get through this if I didn't have your moral support."

Embracing her in return, John wondered if she would have felt that way without the trials that they'd recently had to face. It was an interesting question. One that would bear more consideration. He wasn't ready to assume that bad things had occurred for good reasons but he had no trouble believing that the Lord could use their troubles to bring good in the end.

Those scriptures in the book of Romans had always confused him, yet there were many times when he had seen "all things work together for the good of those who love the Lord and are called according to His purpose."

That was probably the key—the part about being called according to God's purposes. As a human being it was difficult to differentiate between personal desires and what the Lord might want you to do for Him.

In a way, Sam was following that edict when she volunteered to speak for children in court via CASA.

He tightened his arms in a parting squeeze before setting her away and gazing into her eyes. "Don't lose hope, honey. Everything will be okay."

Samantha took a step back before dropping her hands to her sides and smiling wistfully. "From your lips to God's ears, as Elvina used to say."

"We'll be done here soon. Why don't you go keep Lindy company?"

Taking her nod as one of agreement, John started back to speak with his chief where he became embroiled in heated speculation over whether or not Ben Southerland may have arranged the kidnapping and ordered his flunkies to lay down false clues to divert suspicion. That discussion was so absorbing, he failed to notice that Samantha's car was gone until nearly half an hour later.

Returning to the patrol car with the intent of asking Lindy if she knew when Sam had left, he was stunned. The seat was empty. Danny's mother was gone, too.

"Thanks for offering me a lift," Lindy told Samantha.

"No problem. The chief said he was finished with you and me for now. He'll want us to look at pictures of criminals later, but until then we may as well go home. I couldn't see either of us sitting there, stewing and twiddling our thumbs, any longer than absolutely necessary."

"There's more to your kindness than that, I know. And I don't mind. Not really. You've been good to my son and me in spite of all you know about us."

"Danny needed my help and I gave it gladly." She took her eyes off the road long enough to glance at her passenger. The woman's hands were clasped in her lap so tightly that her knuckles were almost white.

"I was just doing what I thought was best," Lindy said softly. "And now look at the mess I've made."

"It's not all your fault. If your husband wasn't involved with criminals Danny would still be with you." She paused to give her words time to sink in before adding, "I think you should tell me everything. Even the smallest detail may help. You must have noticed odd things about Ben's behavior."

"I certainly did." Lindy slewed sideways in the seat so she was facing Samantha. "He's been hard to please for as long as we've been married, but lately he's gotten much worse. It's as if I'm living with a totally different person. Know what I mean?"

"Oh, yes. My father had a Jekyll and Hyde personality, only the change in him was caused by too much alcohol. Does Ben drink?"

"No. Not a drop. Until recently he's seemed pretty happy about everything."

"He changed that drastically?"

Lindy nodded. "Yes. He kept coming home from work more wired than I'd ever seen him and then losing his temper over the stupidest things, like how his steak was cooked or whether Danny remembered his table manners.

It was scary. I never knew what was going to set him off."

"How about his friends? Did they notice anything?"

"Lot of them started avoiding us. I guess they were as puzzled as I was when Ben was so on edge all the time. He had meetings at night, too. Secret meetings. I was supposed to be sleeping but I saw men come and go at odd hours, sometimes two or three times a night."

"Drugs?" Samantha asked.

"If it was, Ben wasn't taking them himself." She shuddered with a stifled sob and chewed her lower lip. "I suppose it might have been that kind of thing. I just don't see how a man like my husband got involved with criminals or what his role could have been. He spent his days sitting in a stuffy office, not roaming around the streets."

"He works as a CPA, right?"

"Not exactly. He's an investment counselor." She named a well-respected firm. "Basically, he tells people how to use their money to make the most profit."

Sam's eyebrows arched and her eyes widened as she made the connection. "Money? That sounds familiar. What did his bosses at work have to say about the fact that he's now a wanted fugitive?"

"They didn't like it a bit when the police contacted them and told them what had happened at the hospital. They sent a representative to interview me right away. When I assured them the incident had nothing to do with Ben's job, they told me I'd better hope I was right because they were going to start an audit of his accounts."

"They did? Do the police know about that?"

Lindy shrugged. "I suppose so. They investigated the firm when they were looking for clues to where Ben had gone, so they must."

"How about you? Do you have any idea where he might be?" The other woman's hesitation told Sam as much as her words would have and she had to bite her tongue to keep from insisting on an immediate explanation.

Finally, Lindy sighed. "There was a summer cabin we used to visit, this side of Mountain View," she said. "I haven't been there in so long I doubt I could find it."

"What about using GPS?"

"You'd have to have coordinates to start with and I have no idea what those might be. All I remember is it was a little way off the main road that leads to Sylamore. It could be anywhere up in the hills. That's really rough terrain and there are a lot of unmarked dirt trails."

"I know," Samantha said. "They don't call it Stone County for nothing. Listen, it's going to be dark in an hour or so but I'm not ready to quit looking. We could head over that way and see if something comes back to you when you see the area. What do you say?"

The forlorn mother seemed to brighten. She smiled slightly. "Do you think we could? Since my car was stolen I have no way to go anywhere on my own. If you don't mind, I'd like to try. Anything to help find Danny."

"My pleasure," Sam said as she turned west. "Just say whatever comes to mind as we drive, even if it seems silly."

"At this point, everything I think or say seems totally irrational," Lindy confessed. "It's as if I'm living a nightmare where I hear Danny calling to me, can't find him and can't wake up, either." She took a noisy, shaky breath. "Do you have children?"

"Not the human kind," Sam said. "I know it isn't the same thing you're going through, but when you love someone or something the way I do, the loss can feel just as unbearable."

"Tell me what happened," Lindy said compassionately as she straightened and adjusted her seat belt across her shoulder. "Maybe listening to your story will help me think more clearly."

"All right. When I was fifteen I saw this poor little puppy being abused and stole him to save his life. That's how it all started."

* * *

John's world had gone spinning out of control the instant he realized he'd lost track of Samantha. If he could have trusted her to have headed straight home he might have worried less. However, she had taken Lindy with her so there was no telling what she was getting herself into.

He immediately tried to phone her and the call went to voice mail. Furious, he pounded his fist into his palm. They had a kidnapping to solve, the sooner the better, and he was having to concern himself with the woman who drove him to distraction on a regular basis. If she had conspired specifically to unhinge him she could not have done a better job of it.

Although he was hesitant to bother Chief Kelso with his personal problems he decided it was wisest to confess. He had expected a gruff reprimand. Instead, Kelso laughed.

"What's so funny?"

"You are, Waltham. I knew how you'd react when you discovered your girlfriend was gone."

"You knew she was leaving? Why didn't you stop her?"

"Stop her? No way. I gave her my blessing when she suggested offering Mrs. Southerland a ride home. Harlan and I figured that woman knew more than she was admitting and would try to sneak off, anyway. Thanks to Samantha, we know exactly where she is. We have an unmarked car following them right now. Don't worry."

"How can you be sure she won't ditch the tail?" John was holding his breath.

"Because there's a bug on her, too."

"Is that legal?"

Levi Kelso arched a brow. "Samantha happened to give us permission. Even if she hadn't, a little boy is missing. If it was your son, Waltham, what would you have done?"

"Bugged her," John replied without delay. "Which way did they go?"

"Toward Melbourne and Sylamore. I take it you intend to head that direction yourself."

"I am off duty, chief. With your permission I'll provide extra backup."

"Sure. You'd do it, anyway," he said wryly. "Just watch yourself. We'll keep you advised by radio. The tracking car Harlan sent has about a half-hour head start but you should be able to overtake it. Adelaide Crowe is driving. She reported that Samantha is taking it real easy, as if she and her passenger are looking for something along the road, so don't go charging up to them and blow the whole operation."

"Gotcha." John was already jogging toward

his truck. He didn't have the benefit of a siren or flashing lights but that was just as well. As the chief had warned, the less attention he attracted, the better.

The chances of those two women finding Danny were slim to none, yet John wasn't ready to write off their efforts quite so soon. Lindy might be directing Samantha, and if that was the case they could actually be successful.

His biggest concern was how involved Sam would get if and when she confronted the men who had snatched the child. She'd already kicked one of them where he lived and was just stubborn and feisty enough to try something equally as dangerous a second time.

Hands fisting on the wheel he put the pedal to the metal and roared out of town.

Saying a prayer occurred to him. He couldn't bring himself to start. He was too worried. Too angry. Surely, God wouldn't take kindly to a plea that came from such an unforgiving heart.

If anything happened to Samantha—his Samantha—he would never forgive himself. Or his chief. Whether Kelso had meant for her to get so deeply involved or not, he hadn't taken steps to stop her.

As far as John was concerned, that was the same as sending an unarmed novice into a cage full of hungry lions.

These were not biblical times and Samantha was not Daniel. The way he saw it, if she got too close to solving the crime, her chances of emerging unscathed were zero to none.

FIFTEEN

Rays from the setting sun were blindingly bright. Squinting, Samantha lowered the driver's side visor.

"How much farther do you think it may be?" she asked Lindy. "We're running out of daylight."

"I don't know." There was a catch in the other woman's voice. "Trying to find the way to the cabin was probably foolish but I just couldn't sit home and wait for news that something terrible had happened to my Danny."

"I know exactly what you mean," Sam said. "I don't think it's at all silly to do whatever we can. We're not hurting anything. Even if there's only a slim chance, at least we're trying."

The police chief had assured Samantha that there was going to be someone discreetly following them, although she hadn't been able to spot any specific car. Considering the serpentine road that led to and from Sylamore, that wasn't very surprising.

She checked her mirrors. Still no visible tail. That might be a bad sign if they actually found the cabin they were looking for. Since they hadn't seen anything that had jogged Lindy's memory so far, however, that was not likely to be a problem. Samantha figured it was enough that she'd gotten the woman to admit to a possible hideout. The police could use that lead to search for both Danny and Ben later.

Weary, she eased the car onto the gravel shoulder of the road as soon as it was wide enough to safely do so. Her hands were cramping from gripping the steering wheel so tightly. She shrugged, rotated her neck and limbered up her arms to help ease painful knots in her muscles.

"We've covered the section of road where you said you thought the cabin cutoff was," Samantha said. "Don't you think we should head back to Serenity? They might have had word about Danny by now."

Lindy nodded slowly, sadly, and pulled her cell phone from her purse with trembling hands. "I gave the police my number. They haven't called."

Her pleading expression and obvious pain touched Samantha's heart. She checked her own cell and noticed a series of missed personal calls—all from John's number. Uh-oh. If he had good news, fine. If he'd been calling merely to chew her out for ditching him—even for a good reason—that was another story.

Choosing to lay aside the phone and reassure her companion before replying to the missed calls she said, "Okay. We'll go a few miles farther. But then we're turning around. It'll be dark before we get home as it is."

Lindy grabbed her hands and held tight, as if she might somehow draw on Samantha's strength. "Thank you so much. I don't know what I'd do if I had to be by myself right now."

"You have friends you can call to stay with you when you get home, don't you?"

"Yes, and no. Like I said before, since Ben got so touchy, a lot of folks have been avoiding us."

"Have you told Brother Logan Malloy about the physical abuse?" Samantha asked gently, mentioning the familiar pastor. The shock she saw on her companion's face made her anticipate a denial.

Instead, Lindy averted her gaze as if embarrassed and shook her head. "No. I haven't told anyone. It wasn't so serious when Ben slapped me, but when he began to hit my son I stood up to him."

"Then how did Danny land in the hospital this last time?"

"I didn't see it coming in time to intervene and Ben…" Lindy cupped her face in her hands and began to sob as if her heart was breaking.

Empathetic, Samantha patted her shoulder, handed her a packet of tissues, sat back and let her cry. There was catharsis in tears. And if anyone was entitled to weep it was this poor woman.

Eventually spent, Lindy sniffled, blew her nose and apologized. "I'm sorry. I didn't mean to lose control like that. I just can't stop thinking about my poor little boy."

"No problem. I've felt like having a good cry myself, more than once, particularly in the past few weeks. Just when it seems things are as bad as they can possibly be, they surprise me and get worse."

"I know what you mean. When Ben's personality changed so radically I didn't know what to do. I suppose I shouldn't have stayed with him but he's my husband. I took holy vows and I want to honor them." She sniffled. "What should I do? I have to protect Danny, too."

"We'll work that out in court," Samantha assured her. "Remember, the judge is your friend. And because I represent Danny through CASA, I'll be able to give the recommendation that he remain with you as long as his father stops hurting him." *Assuming Ben is even in the home after the police get through prosecuting him for hurting John,* she added to herself, hoping that that violent man would get jail time for the assault at the hospital.

"Can you help that much? Really?" There was a glimmer of hope in the young woman's quavering tone.

"We'll see," Sam hedged because she knew she might have jeopardized her CASA assignment by becoming too friendly with Lindy. "The ideal situation is one in which the child stays in the home and the parents get counseling. The court can actually order your husband to participate."

"Oh, that would be wonderful."

"Yes, it would. Are you feeling better now?"

"Much. But plans for the future won't matter until I have my Danny back, safe and sound."

"The police will find him for you. I know they will," Sam said, praying she was right.

She checked her side mirror for oncoming traffic. That's when she saw the unmarked car slowing and pulling off the road behind her. *Speaking of the police. It's about time they showed up.*

Since she didn't want Lindy to lose confidence in her by learning they had been followed by design, Sam decided to walk back and reassure the deputy that all was well. Then she could ask him to report the possibility of a hidden cabin in that area, too, so the rest of the searchers would have clues about where else to look.

She palmed her cell phone and opened the car door. While she was outside she'd be able to return John's calls without being overheard. Hopefully, he'd listen to her explanation before he started to scold.

"Wait right here," she told her companion, forcing a cheery smile. "I think the people behind us may be lost. I'll go see if they need directions."

"Are you sure…?"

Samantha was already out of the car and striding purposefully toward the vehicle idling behind her. It was a good thing that this guy was driving an unmarked car or the subterfuge would have been revealed.

She pushed the button on her phone to return John's calls as she walked. Before one full ring he answered.

"Samantha!"

"Simmer down. I'm fine. Lindy and I are on the road near Sylamore but we're about to turn around and head home. Have you had any word about Danny?"

"No." His voice sounded hoarse, gruff.

"Okay. Don't worry. The cop who's been following us just pulled over. I'm going to go tell him our plans. Then I'll fill you in, too."

"Samantha!" John was shouting. "Did you say *him?*"

"Yes. Hold on a sec."

Not waiting for his reply because she had reached her destination she lowered the phone, paused by the driver's door and watched as the tinted window rolled down.

The man behind the wheel was wearing dark glasses and had a ball cap pulled low in the front so the brim shaded his face. It wasn't a fancy disguise but it was probably all he'd need for his current assignment because it made him resemble nearly every other man in the rural area.

"We're fine," she began, smiling, "just getting ready to head for home. There's nothing to worry about."

He nodded.

"You need to radio your chief for me. Tell him that Mrs. Southerland remembered a mountain cabin where her family used to vacation. It's around here somewhere but she can't recall enough details to get us there."

A wily smile lifted the corners of the man's mouth. "Oh, really?"

Samantha was about to reply when she saw

him raise a gun and point it through the open window. At her!

Hands up, she took a step backward. "Hey! What are you doing? I'm on your side."

"I doubt that," he said, removing his glasses and pushing up the cap brim so she could see more of his face.

"You!" Aghast, she staggered backward. This was no police officer. This was one of the men who had taken Danny. But if he was here, then where was the boy? And what had become of whoever had been in the kidnapping car with them? There had to be at least two more thugs unaccounted for.

He gave a throaty chuckle and flicked the barrel of the automatic at the other car. "Ditch that phone, then yell for your passenger and get her back here, too. We're all going for a little ride in the country."

Although Sam did lower the cell phone and turn the lighted screen to her palm she didn't sever the connection. Her gaze darted from side to side, seeking escape.

"Do you figure you can outrun a bullet, lady? 'Cause if you do, you're crazier than I thought."

"Who *are* you?"

"Obviously not who you'd expected. Now get your passenger to come over here or I'll shoot you where you stand. And her, too."

Given their tenuous situation Samantha saw no choice. At least not a sensible one. If she stalled, hoping that John or the police tail would soon arrive, she might still die for her efforts. If she went with this man, however, he could lead her to Danny.

"Just take me. Nobody else has to be involved."

"Humph. You told me Southerland's wife was with you. That means she has a ticket, too. Now, are you gonna wave at her or shall I?"

"I'll do it."

Mind reeling, body trembling, Samantha made a feeble gesture.

The passenger door of her car swung open. Lindy stood slowly, warily.

"Come here a second," Sam called, hoping she sounded convincing. "And bring my purse, will you?"

"Why?"

The young woman was naturally leery. Anyone would be. Sam half hoped that she'd jump into the driver's seat and speed away. She didn't.

Bending and reaching for Samantha's shoulder bag, Lindy also scooped up her own purse, slammed the car door and started walking toward their shared destiny.

All Samantha could do was stand there, helpless, and watch it happen.

* * *

John was beside himself. He radioed the scant information he had garnered before the signal from Sam's phone had faded. His own lay on the seat beside him, still ostensibly connected to hers, while he used both hands to grip the wheel.

Rounding a particularly tight corner on the winding road he almost clipped the protruding rear bumper of a parked car. Samantha's vehicle was positioned about fifteen yards ahead of it. If he hadn't been looking for it he might have sailed right on past.

He swerved between the two parked cars, slid his pickup to a stop and grabbed his radio. "This is Waltham," he said. "I'm on scene with the Rochard vehicle. I see Adelaide Crowe but there's no sign of a driver or passenger in the other car."

"Affirmative," Levi answered. "Adelaide just told me the same thing. Put your heads together and get back to me with your plans."

"Plans?" John stared at the handheld radio as if it were a poisonous snake. Taking his phone with him he began to jog toward the unmarked sheriff's car.

Dark-haired, slim and ultra efficient, the female deputy met him halfway and nodded a somber greeting. "Motor's still warm," she said, eyeing Samantha's green barge. "I couldn't have missed them by more than a few minutes. Sheriff says you heard her being forcibly taken? Is that right?"

"Yes. She was talking to me." He displayed his own cell phone. "I've lost the signal but if she's still transmitting I may pick it up when we get out of this canyon. Any idea what direction they headed?"

"North. Into the back country." Adelaide pointed at the laptop computer sitting open on the front seat of her car. "The tracking blip is moving fast so they can't be on foot."

"Okay." John was circling to the passenger side of her car as she spoke. "Let's go, then."

"Can't. The sheriff says I'm supposed to stay here and wait for backup."

John tossed her a ring with the keys to his truck, then yanked open the patrol car's door and slid behind the wheel.

"You have your gun and a radio," he shouted. "Now you have wheels. I'm not waiting."

"Hey! You can't take that vehicle. It's the property of the sheriff's department."

"I'll settle with Harlan when all this is over," John yelled through the open window. He gunned the engine, spun the tires and whipped out into traffic, leaving Adelaide standing there with her mouth open.

If this situation hadn't been so dire he might have laughed at her incredulous expression. Instead, he immediately switched his concentration to the computer that was tracking Samantha.

He didn't know how she'd managed to keep the bug with her when she'd left her car but she obviously had. Smart move. Smart woman. He just hoped she hadn't stumbled into a deadly trap.

There was a slight chance that Lindy Southerland was as big a criminal as Ben was. In that case, Sam might be in even more trouble than anyone thought.

The flashing red blip on the computer screen was bearing to the right. John calculated the approximate distance ahead and slowed so he wouldn't accidentally drive into view. It was hard to convince himself to bide his time but he knew he must.

If whoever was with Samantha suspected she was being followed, it could cost her dearly.

He tried to swallow. His throat was so dry he coughed, instead. His fists clenched on the steering wheel, his foot wanting to override his sensibility and depress the gas pedal as far as it would go.

Instead, he cried out to God in a wordless prayer that came from the depths of his soul.

He set his jaw. Squinting into the dimness of the sunset-painted forest, he was able to make out few details. The wind was rising. A storm was brewing.

Only one other thing could have made things worse. Threat of a tornado.

Samantha clutched Lindy's hands as they huddled together in the back of the nondescript sedan and tried to keep from being tossed around when it bounced over massive bumps or dropped into one of the many potholes dotting the dirt track.

The enclosed space reeked of stale cigarette smoke and rotten food. Judging by the fast-food wrappers littering the floorboards, this car served as someone's home away from home—and he was a lousy housekeeper.

"Do you remember any of this terrain?" she asked Lindy in a whisper.

"I don't know. I'm too scared."

"It's okay. They'll find us. I know they will."

The other woman sniffled and squeezed her eyes tightly closed. "I just want my baby back."

The driver snorted derisively. "Your husband should have thought of his family before he double-crossed us."

"I don't know what you're talking about. I

don't know where Ben is or what he's done. I just want to take Danny and go home."

"Yeah, well, that ain't gonna happen unless ol' Ben gets his act together and brings us what we want."

"How is he supposed to know what you want?" Samantha demanded. "Nobody has seen hide nor hair of him since he assaulted a police officer at the hospital and took off."

"Well, you two ladies had better hope he got the word someway because if he doesn't show up with the boss's missing money and prove he's still on our side, he's gonna pay a real high price."

Sam bit her lower lip while Lindy began to sob. There had to be something they could do to escape other than leap from the moving car. Even if they managed to land without injury there was still the problem of eluding an armed man. Plus, they were in the middle of a forest with no map and no idea in which direction safety lay. Fleeing blindly, they could just as easily end up running *to* trouble instead of away from it.

There was only one sensible course of action. Do nothing.

She laid a hand lightly on her purse and prayed that her phone and the tracking device were both working. If not, they were headed for oblivion.

Samantha did believe in God and in the wonders of heaven. She simply wasn't eager to see either in person. Not just yet. Not until she had at least had one more chance to confront John Waltham.

She didn't care how irate he was the next time she saw him as long as there *was* a next time. God willing, she was going to ask John if he still cared as deeply for her as she did for him, then stand back and see what happened.

Yes, it galled her to admit to those tender emotions. And yes, it would mean swallowing a boatload of pride to speak up. But she had to. She just had to.

Beyond that, she prayed that she'd have enough time left to do everything she'd planned before her captors lost patience and carried out their deadly threats.

A shudder zinged through her, head to toe, and her pulse raced, pounding in her temples until her head felt as if it was about to explode.

I'm not ready to give up, Lord, she prayed silently. *And I'm not asking just for myself. Please protect Danny and Lindy.*

A heartbeat later she added, *And Ben. It's not my place to judge, even if I don't like the man—and I sure don't. Forgive me for that and be with us all. Amen.*

SIXTEEN

The blip on the computer screen suddenly stopped moving. John eased the "borrowed" patrol car to a stop and killed the engine so he could listen for distant sounds of human activity. There were none.

Overhead, the sky was rapidly darkening and filling with roiling, black and gray clouds. Not only that, the wind had risen even more, bringing with it a foretaste of the storm to come. Once that arrived he'd be fortunate to hear himself think, let alone pick out voices above the echo of booming thunder.

There was one advantage, however. Although he couldn't hear as well, Sam's abductors would also be far less likely to detect his approach. The biggest question was, where had they taken her and how was he going to steal her back?

One last check of the computer confirmed her stationary position. He checked his phone, found they were still in a dead zone and tossed it aside. It had been clever of her to stay connected. Unfortunately, the trick had failed when the mountain ridges had interfered with transmission. Although that problem was a common one in the Ozarks, it added another dimension to John's distress and made him wish he'd picked a phone service that operated off a satellite feed rather than ground-based towers.

He crouched low beside the sheriff's car and used the radio to report in.

Chief Kelso was not in the best of moods when he realized who was broadcasting. "Are you nuts, Waltham? If you get one scratch on that car it'll come out of your wages. Harlan is on the warpath."

"I have more important things to worry about right now," John said, cradling the microphone so his voice wouldn't carry. "The tracking software shows that our bug is no longer moving. I'll leave this radio on so you can home in on this car. I'm going the rest of the way on foot."

"No, you're not. You're going to stay right there and wait for backup. Adelaide and the others are on their way."

"Copy. That's good to hear."

Kelso's tone moderated. "Hang in there, okay?"

Thunder crashed and boomed, bouncing off the hills and creating a nearly continuous rumble. A flash of lightning made the radio crackle as the bolt shot to ground nearby.

"Sorry, chief, you're breaking up." John grabbed a handful of dry leaves and crumbled them close to his face to add further background noise. "Can't understand a word you're saying."

He tossed the radio microphone back into the car and took a few seconds to check his temporary replacement for the stolen Glock, just as he always did before going into battle. That was exactly what this was, too. They were at war with evil. And he was a soldier on a mission—to rescue at least one special hostage and maybe more.

He wasn't foolhardy. If the situation appeared to require more than one officer he'd wait for help. Unless he thought that doing so would cost someone's life. There were times when a man had to do what he knew was right, no matter how great the likelihood he'd die trying.

John had no death wish. Far from it. But he was not about to sit idly by while Sam remained in jeopardy. His mind might insist that that was the smartest thing to do. His heart disagreed.

He followed his heart.

Samantha could see why these criminals had chosen this particular cabin as their hideout. It was perfect: isolated, hard to reach and impossible to see until you were almost on top of it. Plus, it looked abandoned. If they had brought the car here that they'd used to abduct Danny, they'd hidden it well because she saw nothing to indicate that there was anyone else in the area.

The armed man parked, got out and jerked open the back door. He gestured with the gun. "Out. Both of you. And no tricks."

Samantha moved slowly, purposefully, while her mind continued to search for some logical means of escape. If she'd had only herself to consider she might have made a break for it in the hopes that the thick forest would have given her refuge.

Since she had both Lindy and Danny to think of, she knew better than to try. Even if she did manage to escape, the kidnappers' wrath would surely descend on the remaining captives and Samantha was not willing to put anyone in more peril than they already shared.

As if that were possible, she mused, picking her way across the rock-strewn clearing in the near darkness. Not only was the sun below the horizon, storm clouds had gathered and drifted across the face of the moon, casting a shroud of impending doom as if the entire mountain range was caught up in her personal struggle for survival.

A nearby flash of lightning was followed

mere seconds later by a boom that made Sam jump and prickled the fine hair on her arms and at the nape of her neck.

"Get a move on," their captor shouted, "before we all get toasted."

"It would serve you right," Samantha grumbled without stopping to censor her reaction.

The man huffed. "Very funny. Now stop giving me lip and get in the house before I shoot you where you stand."

Slipping the strap of her purse over her shoulder, she raised her hands enough to demonstrate compliance. She might be too outspoken at times but she was no fool. This was not the time to exert her independence.

The wooden steps creaked as the three climbed them. The door swung open. Bright light from inside made her squint.

Samantha instantly recognized the burly, unshaven man who admitted them. This time, his attitude was even more menacing than it had been when she'd kicked him. Considering their recent confrontation, it wasn't too surprising that he was holding a grudge.

He pointed with the barrel of the small-caliber rifle in his hand. "Inside. Hurry it up."

That was when Samantha looked past him, spotted the little boy and stepped out of the way so Lindy could see him, too.

Danny screamed and ran to his mother the moment he saw her. "Mama!"

Tears gathered in Samantha's eyes. Lindy was clinging to her son and weeping while raining myriad kisses over his face and reddish hair.

"Thank You, Jesus," Sam whispered. The seriousness of their shared situation should not have called for levity, yet she felt a grin begin and let it blossom. Even in such dire straits there was reason for joy, for praising the Lord, and her heart swelled with thanks that the child was apparently unharmed.

Someone gave her a hard shove from behind. Staggering and almost falling, she dropped her purse. It fell to the bare wood floor and spilled some of its contents.

That was enough to cause one of their captors to grab the bag by its bottom seam and upend it. Out slid her cell phone—still obviously connected to her last call!

The man who appeared to be in charge stepped forward and used the heel of his heavy boot to grind the little plastic device to pieces before turning his anger on the one who had brought them to the cabin. "Idiot! Didn't you check? Who was she talking to?"

His cohort shrugged. "I don't know. What does it matter. Ain't no signals up here, anyway."

"For your sake I hope not." He rounded on

Samantha as he kicked the contents of her shoulder bag aside. "I've had just about enough from you. One more stunt like that and you're history, got that?"

She nodded, mute. Her jaw was clenching so hard her teeth were starting to ache. Her cell phone lay in splinters. The bug the police had given her was probably still secure but if anyone actually searched the little pockets inside her purse and found it she was going to be in big trouble—whether it was working or not.

Edging closer to Lindy and the boy, Sam slipped her arm around the other woman's shoulders, drawing moral support as well as giving it. These two brutes were running out of patience and it was only a matter of time before one or both of them snapped.

What could she do? What could anyone do at this point except wait and pray? *Especially pray,* Samantha thought, afraid to close her eyes long enough for even the shortest plea.

Finally, she simply stared at the bare rafters, listened to the rain starting to hammer on the tin roof, and let her heart call out to her heavenly Father with all the anguish she was feeling.

Please, please, Lord, she pleaded, barely able to string words together into a rational sentence. *Help us.*

The picture in her mind was of John Waltham

coming to their rescue like a knight in shining armor mounted on a white horse.

Instead, a gust of wind suddenly caught the cabin door. Sheets of water blew halfway across the unvarnished plank floor, turning a wide swath of it dark.

Both men jumped to their feet, one rushing to close the door and the other pointing his nasty-looking rifle into the opening.

John? Could it be?

Samantha drew a quick breath, preparing to shout a warning.

Before she could call out, Lindy screamed and pressed the boy to her as if sheltering him from even worse danger than they already faced.

A drenched figure stepped into full view, his coat dripping, his light brown hair plastered to his head.

Samantha could hardly believe her eyes.

It was Ben Southerland.

Staying low as he worked his way closer, John thought he heard a woman's high-pitched wail. He froze, listening. Thanks to the storm he was not only getting soaked, he was unable to get an accurate bearing on the noise. It hadn't sounded like Sam's voice but given this complicated situation, there was no way to be certain.

Except to keep going until I can see for my-

self, he added, stepping forward cautiously. He now had the front of a small cabin in sight. Light streamed from the open front door. Someone was silhouetted on the porch.

John pressed his back to the trunk of a broad oak and peeked around. The figure he'd seen was now entering.

The door closed, leaving John in the dark except when a new bolt of lightning flashed and momentarily showed him the way.

"Where are you, Samantha?" he whispered before turning his attention to God. "Where is she? What should I do?"

No booming voice echoed from heaven but he did give thanks for the temporary beacons the storm was providing. It would have been nicer if he could have controlled their light, yet under the circumstances he was grateful for small favors.

The last few strides from the trees to the side of the cabin meant crossing open ground. He scoped out a clear path during a flash, then made the short journey from memory as soon as darkness once again covered his movements.

Breathless, he pressed his back to the rough log wall and fought to control his galloping heartbeat. From that position he could hear snatches of conversation inside the cabin. Most sounded masculine. Nevertheless, it was likely that the building contained at least some of the hostages, if not all of them.

"I didn't double-cross anybody," one man said, his voice rising in panic. "I swear it. I don't know how you guys got that idea."

"Then where's the money you stole?"

"I didn't steal anything. I don't have the account numbers on me right now but all the money you gave me is safe. You need to tell your bosses that. I wasn't hiding anything. I got myself into a little scrape and had to lay low for a while, that's all."

"Some little scrape. Didn't your mama ever tell you not to mess with cops? Of all the people to assault, why pick him?"

"I didn't mean to do it. The guy grabbed my son and I didn't stop to think. It was an accident. After he went down, I guess I lost it. I ran."

With my loaded Glock, John added, positive he now knew the identity of at least one of the occupants of the cabin. *What did you do with it, Ben? Do you still have it? Do you know how to use it? Would you?*

Those questions, although important, were moot until John figured out who else was present.

He edged his way around the side of the building to a small window and slowly straightened.

Lightning flashed. John ducked. At the instant he'd glimpsed Samantha and the Southerlands, it had looked as if one of the occupants of the cabin had been staring right at him! Had he actually been seen? Only time would tell.

Pressed against the side of the cabin he counted the passing seconds. The door in front opened, casting steady light onto the trees directly across the small clearing.

Footsteps thudded on the wooden porch floor.

John tensed. He could hear at least one man approaching but had no idea where any others might have gone. Were more coming? Or had they stayed behind to guard the prisoners?

Another lightning bolt painted John's whole body. It might as well have been the laser sight on a sniper rifle. He saw a shadowy figure swing around.

Instinct made him dive out of the way an instant before a rifle barked. A bullet smashed into the log where his head had been, sending splinters flying.

More shots followed. He was already around the other side of the cabin and heading for the open door when a second gun echoed. John froze. Was that shot *inside?* It sure sounded like it.

Staying low, he scrambled through the doorway, fearing the worst. Someone shot at him. He instinctively returned fire and saw a hefty man stagger, then collapse.

The moment his eyes met Samantha's and he realized she was unhurt in spite of all the gunfire, he felt the weight of the world lift from his shoulders.

A momentary pause to take in the rest of the scene was his undoing.

Sam screamed and pointed. "Look out!"

He started to turn. Something caught him in midmotion and crashed against the back of his head.

Pain! Intense. Blinding. Numbing.

His legs gave out and he crumpled, facedown.

The thud of his body hitting the floor was his last conscious sensation.

Sam gasped. Seeing John knocked out for the second time in as many weeks stunned her, but it was the sharp, cracking sound when the butt of the rifle had connected with his head that was the most ominous. This was no simple faint following a blow. He could easily have been hit hard enough to have fractured his skull. Fatally.

She lunged toward him and was thrown aside by the second kidnapper when he bent to disarm the unconscious officer. Eyes wide, she braced her hands against the floor and stared, watching as the gunman came to the realization that his partner had been shot.

"What the..." His rifle barrel drew an arc

leading to the Southerland family. They had huddled together in a corner while Sam had been attempting to go to John's aid.

The abductor kept his weapon trained on the captives as he knelt beside his cohort. "What happened? Did they jump you?"

"No," the wounded man rasped. "He's got…"

Samantha burst into a series of loud laments, trying to keep the injured man from revealing the full truth.

"See what you've done?" she screeched. "Now what? Huh? This man needs medical attention. Do something! Hurry!"

"You're a nurse. Get over here and take care of him."

"Not him!" she shouted, pointing to John. *"Him!"*

Behind her, she saw Ben Southerland make a subtle shift in his position. There was still one gun the kidnappers didn't know about; one weapon she might be able to count on in a fight. That wasn't much but it was better than nothing.

"I don't care what happens to anybody else," the armed man said flatly. "Take care of my brother."

"Your brother?"

"Yeah. He ain't too bright but he's kin. Now move."

"I'll need bandages and disinfectant and…"

The flash of feral anger in the man's eyes told her she'd pushed him too far. Cautiously getting to her feet, she raised her hands. "Okay, okay. I'm coming."

The older sibling picked up the other's pistol, tucked it into his belt next to the one he'd just taken from John, and stood back to give her room to work.

Samantha knelt next to her patient as he gave a shudder. His full exhalation strongly hinted that any efforts at this point, no matter how heroic, would be futile. Nevertheless, she checked for a carotid pulse. There was none.

So, what would the survivor do when he realized his brother had passed away? she wondered silently. How long could she stall? How was she going to make him think there was still a chance of recovery?

At best, she figured she might be able to fool everybody for a couple more minutes.

She leaned over the dead man and pretended to be staunching the flow of blood from his shoulder wound so she could peek sideways at the other prisoners.

Lindy and Danny were still crouched in the corner, locked in a tight embrace. Ben, however, had worked his way off to one side. Was he planning to fire again? Did he know what he was doing? His first shot had gone wild and if it hadn't been for John's timely arrival they might all have been killed as a result of Ben's feeble attempt at retribution.

"John. Wake up," she whispered.

Although he lay only a few feet from her, he made no response. The only movement that gave her hope was the steady rise and fall of his back as he breathed. As long as that continued it would help her believe that he'd survive.

"Forget him," the armed man ordered. "How is my brother doing? He's not moanin' like he was."

"He's resting," Samantha said. She tried to keep her tone even and hide her fear. Apparently, she was not successful because the remaining gunman leaned over her to get a better look.

She heard him stifle a sob. Then, he staggered backward. "He's *dead*."

"I'm so sorry," she said, meaning every word. "The bullet struck him in a main artery in his shoulder. There was nothing anyone could have done. Not without an immediate transfusion, and even then…"

"Shut up!" He rubbed his eyes using his free hand and waved the rifle erratically with the other. "One of you killed him. I don't care who it was. You're all responsible so you're all going to die."

He pointed the gun at the mother and son cowering in the corner.

Samantha had been preparing to get to her feet. She faltered, dizzy, and wondered if she might faint for the first time in her life.

She nearly did so when he shouted, "Starting with the brat."

SEVENTEEN

What happened next was over in a handful of heartbeats.

Samantha summoned her courage and poised to launch herself toward the gunman. She didn't know what her actual intent was, she simply knew she had to do something to try to protect that child.

The bereaved kidnapper kept swiping wildly at his tear-filled eyes, apparently attempting to clear his vision so he could better pinpoint his targets.

John stirred and moaned at just the right time to offer a distraction.

The kidnapper whirled and braced himself for an attack, wasting no time once he realized that that particular adversary was still unconscious.

He grimaced as he swung the rifle around again and aimed it at the cringing little boy.

Sam saw Lindy lean forward to shield Danny with her body as best she could.

The kidnapper gritted his teeth and pulled the trigger.

Fire erupted from the end of the muzzle. The sharp crack inside the small space was deafening.

Everything blurred as Samantha screamed and lunged forward.

To her surprise, the only pain she felt when she landed was a smarting from the impact of her knees and elbows on the flooring.

Unbelieving, she took stock of herself. She hadn't been shot! So what *had* happened?

She stared at the tableau spread before her. The assailant had fired, all right, but Danny remained unscathed.

Ben Southerland had made a wild dive in front of his family and had taken the bullet meant for the boy. Ben now lay at his wife's feet. Blood was spreading from his wound, soaking through his shirt and pooling on the floor.

Lindy was reaching toward him when he gave a guttural, wordless roar. He raised his head. Faced the gunman. Lifted the stolen Glock in both hands and pulled the trigger for the second time that night.

Samantha was stunned as the bullet flew true and buried itself in the chest of the man who had been trying to kill the child.

The impact threw the target backward. His

rifle flew from his grasp and landed off to the side, no longer a threat.

Samantha was at Ben's side almost before the other man's body hit the floor. She felt for his pulse, then rolled him gently so his face wouldn't be visible to the survivors.

Her gaze met Lindy's. "I'm sorry."

The other woman sagged back against the wall as if her bones had suddenly vanished. That was when Sam noticed that Lindy, too, was wounded. The would-be assassin's bullet had apparently passed through Ben and had grazed Lindy's arm.

"Let me see that," Sam ordered, slipping into her professional persona.

"No." Lindy quickly assessed her whimpering, clinging son, then said, "Danny's okay. That's all that matters. You should tend to your partner. He needs you more than I do."

There was no way Sam was going to argue with that conclusion, particularly since she'd been worried sick about John.

"Okay." She glanced at the other woman's discarded purse. "If you can manage okay, check to see if your cell phone works up here and try to call for help. If you get through, tell them we have an officer down and two wounded."

"What about him?" Lindy pointed with a trembling finger. "Is he dead, too?"

"Yes. He took Ben's bullet square in the chest and he's not bleeding. That means his heart's stopped. We don't have to watch either of these guys anymore."

"Okay." She gave her son a weak smile. "Get Mommy her purse, will you, honey?"

Rather than try to stand when she knew her legs were too wobbly, Samantha crawled the short distance to John and pressed her fingertips against the side of his neck.

She drew a ragged breath and thanked God. Pulse strong, respirations even and deep.

As much as she longed to roll him over onto his back, cradle him in her arms and tell him how much she loved him, she knew better. For his own good he'd have to remain perfectly still until help arrived, unless there was a worsening of his condition.

That sensible conclusion made her smile through tears of relief. Being a nurse was an advantage in most situations but right now she wished she were less aware of correct medical procedures and freer to react to the urgings of her heart.

Placing one hand lightly on his shoulder she continued to monitor his vital signs and silently give thanks for their survival. Everything had happened so fast she was still reeling.

Her hand gently stroked John's upper arm

through his rain-soaked sleeve as she watched the steady rise and fall of his breathing. God was good. Life was good—and promising to get better.

Across the room, Lindy was saying, "That's right. In the mountains. Hold on a second." She covered the phone with her hand. "They want to know if you still have the tracking device on you?"

Sam blushed. "I must. It was hidden in my purse and that's right here."

"Okay," Lindy told the police. "Just follow the signal from whatever it was you gave Samantha Rochard. That should lead you straight to us." Her brow was furrowed. "Yes. We'll be right here waiting for you. We wouldn't think of leaving."

"I did it for Danny's sake," Sam insisted as soon as Lindy laid the phone aside.

Although the injured woman winced when she moved, she did manage a wan smile. "I know you did. It was the right thing to do. I'm just glad I didn't know about it beforehand."

Pulling her sniffling child close again she held him, kissed him and stroked his hair. "We don't know how to thank you, do we, Danny?"

Samantha knew that the dreadful reality of her situation would hit the new widow soon and erase her smile. Once that happened, Lindy was liable to go into shock, which could be more dangerous than her wound, so it would be best to keep her focused on other things for as long as possible.

"Why don't the two of you come over here with me?" Sam suggested, meaning to remove them from proximity to Ben's body.

"If you don't mind, I think I'd like to stay right here for a few more minutes," Lindy said with surprising calm. "We want to say good-bye."

When Samantha saw her begin to speak privately to her son while gazing at the prone figure of the man who had given his life for them, she was in awe. Ben Southerland had been the kind of short-tempered, abusive husband who gave all men a bad name, yet he had come through like a real hero when it had counted.

Sam let tears of sympathy stream down her cheeks without embarrassment. There was good in even the worst people, wasn't there? Above all, she hoped that Danny was able to remember that the last thing his daddy had done for him had shown his love.

John stirred. Moaned. Were those sirens he was hearing in the background? He sure hoped he wasn't dreaming.

His eyelids felt leaden, his ears buzzed. Forcing his eyes open he saw a rough, stained, plank floor and began to recall glimmers of the events that had landed him there. In the deep reaches of his consciousness he thought he remembered hearing shots fired.

Anxious, he started to push himself up, preparing to do battle again if necessary and wondering what had become of the weapon he'd had when he'd burst into the cabin.

Samantha restrained him. "Hold on, mister. You need to lie still. There's no danger anymore."

"What's going on?" Quickly scanning the now quiet room and finding no active threat, he clapped a hand to the back of his head. "Ouch. That hurts."

"I'm not surprised. You took a hard hit," she said, peering into his eyes. "Your pupils are equal and reactive. That's a good sign."

"What about the rest of these men? What did you do, wipe out the whole gang by yourself?"

He saw Sam's smile fade before she nodded toward where Lindy and Danny were.

"No. You and Ben did that. You finished the first man after Ben missed him. Then the other guy tried to shoot Danny and Ben dropped him with a perfect shot. It cost him his life." She sighed noisily. "I think he used the gun he stole from you."

John remained sitting, trying to take it all in

while he waited for a wave of dizziness to pass. "Did you ever figure out what led to all this?"

"I think so. Ben was apparently doing some money laundering for a gang of criminals. When he got into the fight with you at the hospital and ran, they thought he was trying to either cheat them or steal from them and they sent a couple of thugs to settle things. Ben tried to explain himself when he got here but they weren't in the mood to listen."

John grimaced. "A fine hero I am. I came all the way up here to rescue you and missed half the fight."

"You're still my hero," Samantha said with a teary smile. "Always were, always will be."

"Do you mean that?" John was almost afraid to hear her answer but he'd had to ask.

"With all my heart," she said quietly, allowing him to slip an arm around her and draw her closer.

"You've forgiven me?"

"Oh, yes. And I'm not angry at God anymore, either."

"Were you?"

"Yes. I lost faith when I prayed and didn't get the answers I thought I should. It's taken me all these years to realize that most of the problem was my attitude, not what others did or didn't do."

She cuddled closer. "I was a part of something today that I wouldn't have believed if I hadn't seen it with my own eyes. A man I didn't think deserved a second chance, no matter what, stepped up and proved me wrong."

"Speaking of second chances…" John hesitated long enough to lift her chin with one finger so he could see her full reaction as he asked, "Will you marry me?"

"Isn't this a bit sudden?" Her eyes glistened with unshed tears and her grin made her whole face glow as if the sun were rising to illuminate it.

"Not the way I look at it," John said as he prepared to kiss her. "I think we're about five years late."

Samantha slid her arm around his neck and touched her lips to his for an instant before she said, "Better late than never."

The slicker-clad police officers who burst into the cabin ready to do battle were greeted by a knot of survivors. John stepped forward to act as their spokesman.

Samantha deferred to him without argument, especially since he'd confessed to stealing a sheriff's car in order to track her. He'd risked his career for her sake so she figured it would be best if she let him tell the whole story from his point of view.

It was hard to listen without interrupting but she managed to keep quiet. Almost. "There has to be at least one more person involved in this," she added when John paused. "These were the two guys who grabbed Danny outside the hospital but there was another one behind the wheel of the getaway car. I didn't see any sign of him when we got here."

"We've already picked him up," Sheriff Allgood said. "He was dumb enough to drive his own vehicle and leave the real license plate on it. State troopers nabbed him near the Little Rock airport. They think he was planning to fly out of the country."

"So, this was all about money laundering?" she asked. "If so, where was the money coming from? Could it have been from selling drugs?"

John raised his hands as though he'd suddenly found himself on the wrong side of the law and wanted to surrender. "I never told her anything important about our investigation," he said firmly. "She guessed. Honest."

"It's the only conclusion that made sense," Samantha explained. "Ben Southerland managed money and these guys wanted something they thought he'd taken. If not drug profits, then what?"

The sheriff sent her a wry smile. "Are you fishing for a job as a deputy? I may have an opening pretty soon."

Samantha's first thought was that John was going to be fired. Then she remembered that he now worked for the police department instead of Harlan Allgood.

Her brows arched. "An opening? Who's quitting?"

If she hadn't been staring so intently at the sheriff's expression she might have missed the flash of disappointment that lingered only moments before he answered, "Charlie Fox."

"Charlie? Why?"

"I'm not at liberty to say."

Samantha's thoughts whirled. If Charlie was simply moving on to a different job there would be no reason for hedging. Therefore, he had to be in some kind of trouble.

She began to put two and two together. Her forehead knit in concentration. "Wait a second. Charlie was near my house on several occasions when weird things happened." She looked up at John. "He was even there right before we found that last note taped to Brutus's collar."

The sheriff seemed interested. "Really?"

"Yes. Really." Her eyes widened as she realized the importance of what she was implying. "If Charlie was involved with drugs and these guys were, too, maybe there's a connection. Bobby Joe Boland is Charlie's cousin."

Harlan was slowly shaking his head. A lopsided smiled began to lift one corner of his mouth and he directed it at John. "You told me she was sharp. I had no idea how sharp."

He turned his attention to Samantha. "Do you think you can keep a lid on this for a couple more days? I'd hate to have word get out that we were about to conduct a big drug bust and have the rats scatter before we can sweep them up in our trap."

"What about my dog?" Sam asked, both hopeful and anxious. "Somebody still has Brutus. The last warning I got said they'd kill him on Sunday unless I handed over whatever Bobby Joe is supposed to have given me."

"We'll be sure to keep an eye out for your dog," Harlan said. "I can't promise you anything for sure but we'll try our best to get him back for you."

The anxiety of the past few hours had already worn Samantha to a frazzle. Her concern for Brutus added an extra layer of angst. Her heart was heavy, her mood somber.

Then she looked over at Lindy and Danny, put herself in their place and couldn't help feeling ashamed.

She slipped her hand through the crook of

John's elbow and held tight. Many prayers had been answered. There was an enormous amount to be thankful for.

Still, it was all she could do to keep from adding a silent *But...?*

EIGHTEEN

John had participated in the drug raids. All in all, the combined sheriff's and police departments, with the help of the state police, had arrested seventeen criminals from three counties and there were outstanding warrants for more.

That left only one critical task to complete as far as he was concerned. He had to find Brutus. Unfortunately, no one who had been arrested would admit to taking the dog so John had begun cruising the back roads in his free time. It didn't matter how slim his chances were. He had to keep trying. For Samantha's sake.

Reporting that he'd had no success was one of the hardest things he'd had to do in a long time, yet he knew it wasn't fair to keep her hopes up, especially now that Sunday's deadline had passed.

She came out onto the porch as soon as he pulled up in front of her house. Her expression was expectant until he shook his head.

Climbing the steps he reached for her hand, clasping it gently. "I tried my best. None of the raids turned up any clues about Brutus. I'm so sorry, honey."

"It's okay. I'm not very good at accepting *no* as an answer to my prayers but I'm working on it. It's really hard." She sniffled and blinked back unshed tears.

"If there was anything I could do, Sam, anything at all, you know I'd do it."

"I know." She gave his hand a tug. "Come on. Let's sit on the swing out here. It's stuffy in the house."

He let her settle first, then joined her and gave the glider a push to set it in motion as he gazed out across the green, grassy hills and native hardwood forest. "It'll be winter soon. The walnut trees are already shedding their leaves."

"I know. The Purple Martins migrated months ago, too," she added. "I miss their singing, especially in the mornings when I'm getting ready for work. Hearing something cheerful like that would help distract me from what may have happened to Brutus."

The catch in her voice made him slip an arm around her shoulders and pull her closer. Part of him wanted to reassure her that the old dog was fine in spite of suspicions that they'd never see him again. Another urge kept insisting that he offer to buy her a new puppy. Neither seemed right. Not at this point.

Samantha rested her head on his shoulder. "I know life is full of disappointments. I just can't help wishing I had Brutus back. He's already lived longer than big dogs like him are supposed to and I'd like another chance to make his golden years special."

"I doubt he'd have had nearly as long a life if you hadn't come to his rescue when he was little. You gave him a wonderful home and plenty of love."

"But I wasn't done," Samantha protested. "I suppose I'll have to get used to being alone."

"Well, don't get too used to it. You have promised to marry me soon," John reminded her, planting a quick kiss on her hair. "Have you talked to Brother Malloy about performing the ceremony?"

"Yes. You should have seen the expression on his face when I brought it up. He said he's been praying for us for years and…"

When she broke off in midsentence, John was afraid she might be fighting tears again. He was about to reassure her of his undying love when she pushed him away and jumped to her feet.

Mouth agape, eyes wide, she leaned over

the porch railing and used her whole arm to point. "Look!"

At first he didn't see what had gotten her so excited. Then, there was a swaying in the tall weeds that bordered the pasture to the west. He squinted. Noticed a dark shadow. Was he seeing things? If he was hallucinating he wasn't the only one!

Samantha bolted, hammered down the steps and raced across the lawn.

A bedraggled, matted dog with its head held low and tail barely flagging met her at the fencerow.

She fell to her knees and threw her arms around its neck. "Oh, Brutus, where have you been? What happened to you?"

John was grinning from ear to ear as he jogged up to join them. "Too bad he can't tell us. I imagine it's quite a story."

Rocking back on her heels Sam used her hands to do a cursory physical exam. "He's covered with burrs and probably loads of ticks and chiggers but he seems okay otherwise." She lifted the frayed end of a piece of rope that had been looped around his neck. "It looks like he chewed his way loose and escaped."

"Which is probably why nobody would own up to taking him. They didn't have him anymore and hoped they wouldn't be blamed."

Chuckling and sharing her joy, John added, "If you want to give him a bath I'll be glad to stay and help. Either that or you may have to fumigate your house."

"And myself," she said. Grinning broadly she got to her feet and dusted off her clothing. "I don't intend to walk down the aisle at our wedding covered with spots from bug bites."

"I'd marry you even if you had the measles," John said. He started to reach for the frayed end of the cord, then realized how unnecessary that would be. There was no way Brutus was going to leave Sam. Not now. Not after all he'd obviously had to endure to drag himself back to her.

Judging by the old dog's fatigue and the ratty condition of his usually shiny coat, he'd made a long, difficult trek. But he had persevered. And he had made it.

The comparison to their human lives could not have been more crystal clear if Brother Malloy had preached a sermon about it, John thought. He and Samantha had come a long way, too, had endured many trials and had finally found peace, love and forgiveness when they'd been reunited.

Someday he'd share that profound insight with her, John promised himself. Perhaps on their fiftieth anniversary. Right now, they had a dog to wash and plans to make for their future.

The case of Danny Southerland being returned to his mother's custody was easy to bring to a close. Samantha's personal involvement with the family had caused her to be replaced by an unbiased CASA volunteer but their reports had agreed. Since Lindy was now a widow there was no longer a threat of abuse. Therefore, the child would be safe in the family home and a judge had so ruled.

Lindy held her son's hand and grinned at Sam as they exited the courtroom. "Thank you so much."

"I was glad to be able to help. Is there anything else I can do for you? I know it has to be difficult right now."

"Not as bad as I thought it might be," the young mother said. "Ben had some life insurance that paid double for an accidental death, and the people at his firm have been very helpful—in spite of his foolishness." She cast a sidelong glance at her son. "We're adjusting well, I think."

"I'm glad."

"I heard at church that you and John Waltham are planning a wedding. Congratulations. When's the big day?"

"Next month." Sam felt a smile lift one corner of her mouth higher than the other and had to laugh at herself. "I can't believe how nervous I am. I grew up in a dysfunctional family and there are times when the idea of getting married terrifies me."

"Don't be scared," Lindy said. "I know there must be many couples who are blessed to be together."

They fell into step and headed down the hallway of the courthouse. "What about you?" Sam asked. "Do you think you might ever remarry?" The astonished expression on Lindy's face made her chuckle.

"Okay," Sam said, "maybe it's a little too soon for that question. Sorry."

"My first and only duty now is as Danny's mother," Lindy vowed. "He's been through enough trauma to last a lifetime. I'm certainly not planning to shake up his world, or mine, by getting involved in a romance." She smiled. "I think that kind of thing is overrated anyway."

Samantha laughed lightly. "I sure hope not. I've waited a long time to see my dreams come true."

"Then I wish you the best."

Lindy offered her hand and Samantha took it. "You, too. God bless you."

"He already has," Lindy said, turning an adoring gaze on her son. "Thank you for getting my son back for me."

When Sam replied, "My pleasure," she meant it with all her heart.

The wedding had been planned as a small, informal affair and had rapidly grown to include the entire congregation of Serenity Chapel and many of the law enforcement officers John had worked with over the years, as well as a small group of representatives from CASA.

Finally, the bride and groom had simply given up and had thrown the event open to all by extending a blanket invitation the way so many country folks did.

John's biggest concern was whether or not Sam's parents would attend and if they did, what her reaction might be. He wanted the day to create the kinds of memories she would cherish, not be something she hated to recall.

He needn't have worried. By the time of the service, Brother Logan Malloy and his wife, Becky, had taken care of everything. The flowers were arranged perfectly. Candles graced the altar. The main aisle was covered in a white runner and the organist had a list of the special music Samantha had selected.

There was one more astounding element. Not only had Sam's estranged mother returned to town to attend the ceremony, Brother Malloy had refereed a family reunion of sorts and Samantha's father was set to walk her down the aisle.

This breakthrough didn't mean that all their past differences had been settled and all the hurt erased, but it was a good start.

John was waiting at the front of the sanctuary with his best man, Chief Kelso, when Samantha stepped into view.

The congregation stood and turned to watch her approach. Her gown was simple yet elegant, her veil as light as butterfly wings floating around her head and shoulders.

The moment John saw her radiance and watched her take her father's arm, he knew. This was not merely an act of obedience to tradition, she had truly forgiven. There was nothing more he could ask for her sake.

For himself, he prayed fervently that he would be the kind of husband who made Samantha proud to be his wife.

Her gaze met his and held it. She smiled.

John's heart was galloping and he felt himself sway slightly.

One more slow step. Then another. And another.

She released her father's arm and reached out to John.

He took her hand.

They turned to face the altar, together, as the music faded away.

The pastor cleared his throat. "Dearly beloved…"

* * * * *

If you liked this book, be sure to look for STANDING GUARD, the next story in Valerie Hansen's series THE DEFENDER, *coming in September, only from Love Inspired Suspense.*

Dear Reader,

Many of my books end up dealing with forgiveness, whether I plan it that way or not, and I often find myself wondering what God may be trying to tell me.

In the case of CASA, I've learned that there are large groups of selfless individuals who put themselves second in order to help innocent children obtain justice. I cannot imagine a more worthy goal. Or a more heart-wrenching task.

Whatever the Lord has given you or me to do in this world, I pray that we will do it with grace and joy. Help is always just a prayer away. All we have to do is ask.

If you wish to contact me, the fastest way is by email. My address is VAL@VALERIEHANSEN.COM or you can send a letter to P.O. Box 13, Glencoe, AR 72539. To see a list of my books, past and future, just go to VALERIEHANSEN.com.

Blessings,

Valerie Hansen

Questions for Discussion

1. This story begins with an unexpected reunion. Is it natural for Samantha to greet John with anger when he once held such a special place in her life? Can you understand her viewpoint?

2. In the years they've been apart, both Samantha and John have changed. Do you think this separation would have been as big a problem for them if they had remained together?

3. As the story develops, Samantha admits she was angry at God as well as at John after he left town. That's a normal reaction to not getting the answers to prayer that we expect. Have you ever had to battle those kinds of feelings?

4. A career of service to others is exemplified by both Samantha's and John's professions. Given their past, can you see what those choices were based upon?

5. Drug problems are not limited to big cities. Did it surprise you to learn that people in small, rural communities share the same ordeals?

6. Opal is a grandmother who helped raise her grandchildren. Do you think she did the right thing? Did she really have a choice or was the responsibility thrust upon her?

7. Samantha is very attached to her old dog, Brutus, and thinks of him as family. Have you ever had a beloved pet who seemed to understand you better than other people do?

8. There are instances in this story when the characters choose to break rules because they believe they are in the right. Was this wrong? Why or why not?

9. When Samantha stopped going to church, she told herself it was because John had left. Is what someone else has done a good enough reason to stop having fellowship with other believers?

10. Can you picture an area in the mountains that is so remote it's rarely visited? Would that be the best place to hide a kidnap victim or would it be easier to blend in where there are crowds?

11. Ben Southerland's personal problems caused him to lash out at his family. Would he have been able to regain his family's trust or was

it too late? Why is it never too late for God's forgiveness? (I John 1:9)

12. It takes the threat of possible separation via death to awaken Samantha to the full extent of her love for John. How different might her life have been if she had accepted his offer of marriage when she was much younger?

13. A lot of healing takes place before the wedding. Is it wishful thinking to imagine that Samantha can forgive her repentant father enough to include him in her life again? Will it be easier for her to reach out to others now that she has John by her side and they share the support of their church family, as well?

LARGER-PRINT BOOKS!

**GET 2 FREE
LARGER-PRINT NOVELS
PLUS 2 FREE
MYSTERY GIFTS**

Love Inspired®
SUSPENSE
RIVETING INSPIRATIONAL ROMANCE

Larger-print novels are now available...

YES! Please send me 2 FREE LARGER-PRINT Love Inspired® Suspense novels and my 2 FREE mystery gifts (gifts are worth about $10). After receiving them, if I don't wish to receive any more books, I can return the shipping statement marked "cancel". If I don't cancel, I will receive 4 brand-new novels every month and be billed just $4.99 per book in the U.S. or $5.49 per book in Canada. That's a saving of at least 23% off the cover price. It's quite a bargain! Shipping and handling is just 50¢ per book in the U.S. and 75¢ per book in Canada.* I understand that accepting the 2 free books and gifts places me under no obligation to buy anything. I can always return a shipment and cancel at any time. Even if I never buy another book, the two free books and gifts are mine to keep forever.

110/310 IDN FEH3

Name	(PLEASE PRINT)	
Address		Apt. #
City	State/Prov.	Zip/Postal Code

Signature (if under 18, a parent or guardian must sign)

Mail to the **Reader Service**:
IN U.S.A.: P.O. Box 1867, Buffalo, NY 14240-1867
IN CANADA: P.O. Box 609, Fort Erie, Ontario L2A 5X3

Not valid for current subscribers to Love Inspired Suspense larger-print books.

**Are you a current subscriber to Love Inspired Suspense books
and want to receive the larger-print edition?
Call 1-800-873-8635 or visit www.ReaderService.com.**

* Terms and prices subject to change without notice. Prices do not include applicable taxes. Sales tax applicable in N.Y. Canadian residents will be charged applicable taxes. Offer not valid in Quebec. This offer is limited to one order per household. All orders subject to credit approval. Credit or debit balances in a customer's account(s) may be offset by any other outstanding balance owed by or to the customer. Please allow 4 to 6 weeks for delivery. Offer available while quantities last.

Your Privacy—The Reader Service is committed to protecting your privacy. Our Privacy Policy is available online at www.ReaderService.com or upon request from the Reader Service.

We make a portion of our mailing list available to reputable third parties that offer products we believe may interest you. If you prefer that we not exchange your name with third parties, or if you wish to clarify or modify your communication preferences, please visit us at www.ReaderService.com/consumerschoice or write to us at Reader Service Preference Service, P.O. Box 9062, Buffalo, NY 14269. Include your complete name and address.

LISUSLP11B